SINGLE STATUS

Linda Swift

Whimsical Publications, LLC

Florida

Single Status is a work of fiction. Names, characters, and incidents are the products of the author's imagination and are either fictitious or are used fictitiously. Any resemblance to actual events or persons, living or dead, is entirely coincidental.

To purchase the authorized electronic edition of *Single Status*, visit
www.whimsicalpublications.com

Cover art by Traci Markou
Editing by Melissa Hosack

Published in the United States by
Whimsical Publications, LLC
Florida

ISBN-13: 978-1-936167-44-9

Printed in the United States of America

ACKNOWLEDGEMENTS

With thanks to Bob whose power plant knowledge and golf
expertise made this book possible.

A deeply tanned man of indeterminate origin rushed in and seeing the group, came to stand in their midst.

"Are you guys here with IPPS?" he inquired, and when they nodded, he went on. "Good. I'm Albert Zurow, your operations supervisor." He glanced at each of them in turn, then reached into his shirt pocket for a crumpled piece of paper. "We'll get started and hope the other plane arrives before long." He nodded toward the first person to his left. "And you are?"

"Carl Evans." The man was short, had a protruding paunch and a receding hairline. B.J. guessed him to be over forty.

"Pete Marshall here." This one looked younger and in health club workout condition.

The introductions continued around the circle. "I'm Frank Kelly." Only three words but said in a tone of self-importance that was irksome.

"Yancy Webb." Adjusting his glasses, he straightened his lanky frame.

"Next, please." Albert Zurow looked impatiently at the man to his immediate right.

"Oh, sorry. Dana Thomas." Tall, dark and handsome, and he was probably well aware of it, B.J. observed silently.

Zurow consulted his list. "Sutherland's plane must be late. I'll just—"

"I'm here." B.J. took a reluctant step toward the group. Six heads turned at the sound of B.J.'s voice. Six pairs of eyes stared in silence. Then Zurow recovered enough to speak.

"You're a woman," he said accusingly.

"Well, so I am." She gave the astonished man a wry smile and waited expectantly.

"There must have been some mix-up at the stateside headquarters. Nobody mentioned this, and the resumes haven't been received yet so—"

"Is there some restriction against female employees here?" B.J. asked with a delicate lift of one eyebrow.

Zurow blanched as though he envisioned an army of feminists already marching in picket lines around the plant site. "No. No, of course not. ChemCorp is an equal opportunity employer. It's just that we have arranged for the men, uh, employees to share housing and transportation in pairs. We've already leased every available villa in the area and now..." He looked at B.J. and shrugged.

"I have no problem with this," she told him calmly.

"I don't have a problem with it either," Carl Evans commented with a worried frown, "but I think my wife would."

"Anyone else here married?" Zurow asked.

"Guilty." Yancy Webb shook his head regretfully.

Zurow cleared his throat and looked back toward the circle of men surrounding him. "Each villa has two bedrooms," he said in a placating tone, "so only the bath would be jointly shared."

"We could draw straws." Frank Kelly smirked as he looked at the other two men.

"Or somebody could volunteer," Pete Marshall said with a meaningful look at Kelly.

"We're assigning pairs to alternate shifts," Zurow continued after an awkward silence, "so there would be plenty of privacy." He looked from one man to the other, his patience clearly wearing thin.

"Come on, fellas," B.J. chided, "this is the twenty-first century. I don't have anything contagious. I won't hang pantyhose in the shower. Actually, I don't even wear pantyhose. And I promise not to make a pass at whoever is brave enough to share quarters with me."

Kelly rolled his eyes, and Marshall nudged him. "Want to flip for it?"

Dana looked from the two men to the woman who stood waiting in her neatly creased tan slacks and white tailored shirt. Her hair was the color of ripe wheat, and she wore it in a short, boyish cut which made it hard to miss the bright splotches of color on her high cheek bones. She was obviously embarrassed by the situation but determinedly holding her ground and keeping it light. At the rate things were going they'd still be here tonight arguing about who had to make the supreme sacrifice of bunking with a good-looking woman. If he solved the problem, they could move on to the business of settling in.

"I'll do it."

Six pairs of eyes turned toward him, four registering surprise and the other two gratitude. Dana felt himself turn red as he reached down and picked up his briefcase. "So let's get on with it."

CHAPTER ONE

Above the clear aquamarine waters of the Caribbean, the Boeing 737 began its slow descent toward St. Croix. B.J. Sutherland glanced again at the assignment letter from International Power Plant Specialists classifying the job as temporary single status. But as far as B.J. was concerned there was nothing temporary about being single. With a little luck and a lot of effort, temporary could lead to negotiation of a permanent contract but the status of single was nonnegotiable. Folding the piece of paper and slipping it back into a slim briefcase which still smelled of new leather, B.J. methodically obeyed the fasten seat belt instructions and prepared for landing.

On another glide path toward the same destination, Dana Thomas studied an identical letter and sighed. Everything was temporary except single status and that was forever. After almost two years it still was a term that fit unnaturally—like wearing another person's shoes. The job in Saudi had ended badly and this was a chance to make amends. There was only so much slack allowed for recovery and then expectations reverted to normal. The jet's engines whined as it came in low for landing and Dana stuffed the letter into a well-worn briefcase and tightened his seat belt just as a sign above blinked its automatic message.

The Alexander Hamilton Airport was bustling with passengers arriving and departing and even with its air-conditioned interior, the muggy tropical heat rushed in each time the outside doors were opened. To one side of the Hertz Car Rental counter, a cluster of five men surreptitiously eyed each other without speaking. B.J., standing a little behind the others, adjusted the straps of a new canvas backpack and waited with growing apprehension.

A deeply tanned man of indeterminate origin rushed in and seeing the group, came to stand in their midst.

"Are you guys here with IPPS?" he inquired, and when they nodded, he went on. "Good. I'm Albert Zurow, your operations supervisor." He glanced at each of them in turn, then reached into his shirt pocket for a crumpled piece of paper. "We'll get started and hope the other plane arrives before long." He nodded toward the first person to his left. "And you are?"

"Carl Evans." The man was short, had a protruding paunch and a receding hairline. B.J. guessed him to be over forty.

"Pete Marshall here." This one looked younger and in health club workout condition.

The introductions continued around the circle. "I'm Frank Kelly." Only three words but said in a tone of self-importance that was irksome.

"Yancy Webb." Adjusting his glasses, he straightened his lanky frame.

"Next, please." Albert Zurow looked impatiently at the man to his immediate right.

"Oh, sorry. Dana Thomas." Tall, dark and handsome, and he was probably well aware of it, B.J. observed silently.

Zurow consulted his list. "Sutherland's plane must be late. I'll just—"

"I'm here." B.J. took a reluctant step toward the group. Six heads turned at the sound of B.J.'s voice. Six pairs of eyes stared in silence. Then Zurow recovered enough to speak.

"You're a woman," he said accusingly.

"Well, so I am." She gave the astonished man a wry smile and waited expectantly.

"There must have been some mix-up at the stateside headquarters. Nobody mentioned this, and the resumes haven't been received yet so—"

"Is there some restriction against female employees here?" B.J. asked with a delicate lift of one eyebrow.

Zurow blanched as though he envisioned an army of feminists already marching in picket lines around the plant site. "No. No, of course not. ChemCorp is an equal opportunity employer. It's just that we have arranged for the men, uh, employees to share housing and transportation in pairs. We've already leased every available villa in the area and now..." He looked at B.J. and shrugged.

"I have no problem with this," she told him calmly.

"I don't have a problem with it either," Carl Evans commented with a worried frown, "but I think my wife would."

"Anyone else here married?" Zurow asked.

"Guilty." Yancy Webb shook his head regretfully.

Zurow cleared his throat and looked back toward the circle of men surrounding him. "Each villa has two bedrooms," he said in a placating tone, "so only the bath would be jointly shared."

"We could draw straws." Frank Kelly smirked as he looked at the other two men.

"Or somebody could volunteer," Pete Marshall said with a meaningful look at Kelly.

"We're assigning pairs to alternate shifts," Zurow continued after an awkward silence, "so there would be plenty of privacy." He looked from one man to the other, his patience clearly wearing thin.

"Come on, fellas," B.J. chided, "this is the twenty-first century. I don't have anything contagious. I won't hang pantyhose in the shower. Actually, I don't even wear pantyhose. And I promise not to make a pass at whoever is brave enough to share quarters with me."

Kelly rolled his eyes, and Marshall nudged him. "Want to flip for it?"

Dana looked from the two men to the woman who stood waiting in her neatly creased tan slacks and white tailored shirt. Her hair was the color of ripe wheat, and she wore it in a short, boyish cut which made it hard to miss the bright splotches of color on her high cheek bones. She was obviously embarrassed by the situation but determinedly holding her ground and keeping it light. At the rate things were going they'd still be here tonight arguing about who had to make the supreme sacrifice of bunking with a good-looking woman. If he solved the problem, they could move on to the business of settling in.

"I'll do it."

Six pairs of eyes turned toward him, four registering surprise and the other two gratitude. Dana felt himself turn red as he reached down and picked up his briefcase. "So let's get on with it."

"Very good, Thomas." Zurow stepped quickly to the counter and with a few words procured three sets of car keys. "Here we go, then. Evans, a set for you and—"

With a quick look at the other married man, Carl Evans supplied a name. "Webb."

"So that leaves Marshall and Kelly together, I presume?" When they both nodded, Zurow gave another set of keys to the latter. He handed the remaining set to Dana Thomas.

"I'll meet you at the administration building in the morning at seven sharp. Check your assignment letter for directions to the plant site." He looked around the circle. "Any questions?" When there was no response, he went on, "Now if you will just collect your luggage and follow me, we'll be on our way to Christiansted. In case anyone gets lost in traffic, our destination is Schooner Bay. And remember, you are driving on the left side of the road."

At the luggage carousel, Dana turned to B.J. "How many bags do you have?"

"Two."

"What color?"

Now it dawned on her. He expected to help her! Ignoring the question, she said decisively. "I can manage, thank you."

"Whatever you say." He jerked his own large beat up khaki bag from the conveyer and turned away, leaving her to wait what seemed an interminable time for her own matched pair of black American Touristers to appear.

Hitching the straps of her backpack more securely and tucking her briefcase under one arm, she lifted the other two bags and made her way toward the door just as Dana disappeared through it.

The heat and bright sunlight slammed into her like an invisible wall, but B.J. pushed on. She caught up with him in the parking lot but was too winded to speak, so they proceeded to the row of cars in silence.

He unlocked the trunk of a dark green Ford Escort and fitted his large bag inside. He then turned to reach for hers, but she shook her head.

With effort, B.J. hoisted first one bag, then the other into the space that was left. She tossed her backpack and briefcase onto the back seat.

He didn't offer to let her drive, she noted as she climbed into the passenger's side and fastened her seat belt. Well, she hadn't really expected him to.

Dana backed the car out of the parking space and gave his attention to following the caravan ahead of them. The wide highway soon gave way to a more narrow one, and the flat terrain became a series of sharp curves and hills.

"I guess I ought to say thank you," she told him after they had driven in silence for a few minutes.

"For what?" he asked curtly. "You carried your bags."

"Not the bags. For agreeing to bunk with me." Somehow the words seemed to convey more than she had intended, and she didn't want him to get the wrong idea. B.J. took a deep breath and went on. "I think we ought to get this straight from the beginning. I'm not looking for anything, you know, like..." Her voice trailed off as his dark eyes left the road and bored into hers.

"Neither am I, so you can rest easy on that score."

"Good." She shifted slightly in her seat and focused on the highway, praying that he had, too, because another treacherous curve loomed just ahead of them. When they were safely around it, she went on. "And I don't want you to think I expect you to make any special allowances for me. Just treat me like— like—"

"Just another guy?" he finished for her.

"Yes, that's it."

"Okay, B.J. You've got it." His tone made her glance at him, but his expression gave no hint of amusement, so she had to assume he had taken her as seriously as she had intended. "Why did you do it?" she asked suddenly.

This time he didn't pretend to misunderstand the question. "I guess I'm just a sucker for losers."

"I'm not a loser," she snapped. "Just because I'm a woman doesn't mean—"

"Whoa. It wasn't intended as a putdown of women. You seemed to be slightly outnumbered back there, so let's just say I have a weakness for the underdog."

"Thanks."

"Don't mention it."

B.J. settled back in her seat and stole a surreptitious glance at the driver. His dark good looks and angular, clean-cut profile might have been attractive if she entertained such thoughts, but she didn't. Her attraction for the opposite sex was as dead as her ten-year marriage, and she planned to keep it that way.

The car rounded another curve, and Schooner Bay with its jumbled array of colorful boats lay before them. The deep blue water of the sheltered inlet sparkled in the late afternoon sun, and B.J. felt as though she was looking at a travel poster. "It's beautiful, isn't it?" she said softly.

"What?" When she gestured toward the bay, Dana nodded without enthusiasm.

"Of course, this is my first assignment outside the States. I guess you've been all over."

"Yeah."

Whatever else the man might be, he couldn't be accused of being too talkative, B.J. decided.

They were climbing away from the bay now and approaching the cluster of pastel stucco villas where they would be living. Dana slowed the Ford, and they looked for the house number corresponding to the keys they had been given. Theirs was the building at the top of the hill with a stunning view of the bay below.

A profusion of vivid Bougainvillea spilled over the wrought-iron fence that enclosed the stone-paved courtyard. It was secured by a locked gate, and iron bars covered the low windows. B.J. felt a moment of dread at the thought of spending hours alone here, but she quickly forced it aside.

The villa's interior was light and airy with white ceramic tiled floors and pastel walls. Vivid oil paintings on varying sized canvas frames depicted island scenes. They put down their luggage inside the hallway and looked at each other.

"You can choose." Dana indicated the bedrooms on either side with their white wicker furniture and shuttered windows. Bold floral designs on bedspreads and chair cushions reflected the island décor. Plush shag rugs matched the fabrics. One room contained twin beds, the other a double.

"I'll take this one," B.J. said and quickly moved to claim the room with single beds.

"Fine."

Depositing their bags, they inspected the rest of the

house, beginning with the bath opening off the hall.

"You take the drawers and medicine chest," Dana offered.

"No, I'll take half," B.J. said adamantly, "of both, but since you're taller, I'd like the lower shelves please."

"But I won't need as much space as you," Dana insisted stubbornly.

"It doesn't matter. Fair is fair." B.J. crossed her arms and glared at him.

"Just one of the guys. I temporarily forgot. Sorry."

He looked more irritated than sorry, but B.J. let it pass. She didn't suppose he'd ever had the misfortune to be paired with a woman before and he had been nice enough to agree to it. He'd also averted the crisis that seemed to have been developing back at the airport. Men could be so dense. They acted as if females were a different species instead of a differently equipped version of themselves. She had already proven that she was just as capable as any man in the training program, but would continuously have to prove it again on every job. Women had to work twice as hard as the men just to prove they could cut it.

She and Dana moved on to the modern kitchen that was separated from the dining and living areas by an island counter. The bamboo and glass furnishings with their tropical print cushions in cool pastel colors created an airy sense of space. That feeling was extended by a glass wall with sliding partitions that opened to a wide veranda, screened and barred. B.J. couldn't decide whether she felt safe or imprisoned by the impenetrable enclosure. "I've just realized the house is open to the heat but it feels cool, like air-conditioned," B.J. said with surprise.

"It's the trade wind," Dana said.

She stepped closer to the screen and looked beyond at the vast expanse of water stretching to meet the horizon. What a romantic vista. Now why did thoughts like that keep popping into her head? It must have something to do with the close proximity of the undeniably handsome man who stood behind her, although a man hadn't affected her that way in a very long time. She'd have to get a grip on her fantasies before she gave Dana Thomas the wrong signals. Though from what she had observed so far, he seemed immune to her signals entirely. So much the better.

"I guess we should get in some supplies before we report to the job." He gestured toward the kitchen. "Would you like to take turns at KP?"

"No, I wouldn't," she answered decisively.

"Okay, then, every man for himself," he told her affably, and she detected a slight grin before he looked away.

"I'm sure we'd have different tastes," she went on, "so it just wouldn't work."

"Fine." There was an amused glint in his eyes when they met hers. "Do you have any objections to shopping together, or is that also on your list of shalt nots?"

"My what?" B.J. did a slow burn. "Look, I just think it's important to establish some ground rules here, like the fact that I don't do kitchen duty for both of us."

"I never said—" he began, but she cut him off.

"And I don't do laundry or clean for anyone but myself."

"Fair enough." He looked around him. "So we'll each clean our own bedrooms and split the rest of the villa in half? Which half of the bath do you prefer to sanitize?"

"It's not necessary to be sarcastic. I'm sure we can work out some equitable arrangement for cleaning. Perhaps alternate weeks, except for the bedrooms, of course."

"Of course," he nodded solemnly. "Now about those groceries. We need to get going, don't you think?"

"Yes," she held out her hand with an air of impatience, "and this time I'll drive if you don't mind."

"Would it matter if I did?" he asked morosely.

"No, it wouldn't," she snapped. Taking the keys and heading for the door, she wondered how long it was going to take Dana Thomas to understand that his house-mate was a twenty-first century woman and not some helpless airhead he could play benevolent dictator to. She reminded herself to be grateful that he had volunteered to share a villa with her but that didn't mean it was going to be easy living with him. She'd never expected to live with any man again, even on a job. Something told her this was going to be a very long temporary assignment.

CHAPTER TWO

B.J. quickly realized that buying groceries at the nearest supermarket would prove to be more of a challenge than shopping stateside. Fresh produce was disappointing in both quantity and quality, canned goods were scant, meat looked questionable, and the prices had deflated her allotted budget. When she reached the check-out counter, Dana was already waiting with a bulging bag of his own.

With dairy items that needed to be kept cool against the oppressive heat, they had to return to the villa as quickly as possible. B.J. blamed that for her near-miss when she took a curve too fast. In truth, she almost forgot and swung to the wrong side of the highway, but she'd never admit it to the smug man beside her who was probably gloating at her embarrassment.

After they unpacked and stored their respective supplies, Dana asked, "Would you like to go someplace for dinner?"

B.J. shook her head. "No, thanks. I'm tired. I'll just fix something here."

"I could head back to the nearest fast food place and get a takeout order for both of us," he offered.

"You don't have to concern yourself with me, Thomas," she told him emphatically.

"Look, Sutherland," he answered, taking her cue and addressing her by last name, "I'd suggest the same to anyone. It's no big deal. In fact, I'd kinda like to kick off my shoes and relax, too. It's been a long day."

"If you let me pay half," she said reluctantly.

"By all means." He took the bill she held out and shoved it in the pocket of his faded, well-cut jeans.

After he left, B.J. rummaged in the cabinets for cutlery and stoneware and set the table. Dana Thomas was a thoughtful guy, she'd give him that. She only hoped he wasn't making concessions to her because she was a woman. Well, this kind of thing wasn't likely to happen again since they'd be on opposite shifts as soon as their orientation was over. Belatedly, she realized that he hadn't even asked her what she'd like to eat, and her opinion of him did a hundred and eighty back to square one.

When Dana returned, darkness had fallen and the villa was aglow with soft lights, reminiscent of other homecomings. He had with him a large pizza and a bottle of red wine. Maybe his house-mate would get the wrong idea and think this was leading to a big seduction scene, but that was her problem. It wasn't that she was bad looking. In fact, she was just the opposite in spite of her effort to be one of the boys. But she had a chip on her shoulder as wide as a two-by-four, and she was as sensitive as an abscessed tooth. Come to think of it, she was developing into a real pain in a cavity lower than his mouth. Playing the Good Samaritan back there at the airport was already causing him to have misgivings. He wasn't used to having his space invaded, and sharing quarters with anyone would have been a strain, so why had he confounded the problem by taking on a female who obviously had big problems with gender identification? He wondered idly if she'd ever been married and quickly vetoed the idea. She was clearly out to best men, not bed them.

Opening the car door, he stood for a moment feeling an unexpected yet familiar anticipation at what awaited him in the lighted villa. Kate should be coming to the door at the sound of his key, and he would enfold her in a warm embrace. He would kiss her forehead, which reached just even with his mouth, and before she could lift her face for a real kiss, Jared would come running. The little boy would be shouting for attention, and he would bend to swoop him up and carry him back inside. Dana slammed the door with more force than necessary and went to face the empty reality inside the villa where a stranger waited.

B.J. stood on the shaded veranda taking deep, measured breaths of the fresh sea air. Below her the first rays of the sun shot the dark aquamarine water with streaks of lighter hues. Palmetto palms clung to the steeply sloping hillside that was dotted with blooming red and yellow frangipani. Nearby a small flock of bananaquits argued noisily over a coveted morsel of food. B.J. was so engrossed in her thoughts that she was scarcely aware of the sights, sounds, and scents of the tropical paradise that surrounded her.

She was scared. This job meant a lot to her and not only as a means of proving herself and insuring her future with IPPS. It would also prove to Tom Sutherland that she wasn't the brainless parasite he'd almost succeeded in creating in the ten years of their marriage. She had married Tom right out of high school, and then taken a low paying job to help him through the training program with IPPS. After that, he hadn't wanted her to work, and like a fool, she'd acquiesced. With constantly moving from place to place, there'd been little choice in the matter anyway. Now, she was on her own and if she failed...

A sound from the kitchen interrupted her thoughts, and B.J. turned to offer her house-mate a friendly good morning. The words stuck in her throat at the sight of the slightly tousled man whose day-old growth of beard only added to his dark, brooding good looks. He was wearing a pair of wrinkled sweat shorts and a white tee shirt which made him look even taller than she remembered. It had been a long time since she'd seen a man before breakfast. She had almost forgotten how appealing that could be.

He looked from the cup she held to the empty coffee pot with a puzzled frown. "Coffee?" he asked hopefully in a slightly raspy voice even as she shook her head.

"I wasn't sure how you like it," she explained, "so I made only enough for one." She shrugged and drained her cup, wondering why she should feel apologetic.

"Any way at all, preferably black and quick," he ground out as he jerked on the faucet and filled the pot.

Appeased by the aroma that promised quick gratification, Dana looked at the woman silhouetted against the rising sun.

She had substituted Levis for her creased khakis. The way the new pants molded to her soft curves, there was no mistaking her for just one of the guys. As he studied her womanly form, Dana felt an unfamiliar sensation of longing and expelled a soft oath under his breath. Maybe being the Good Samaritan wasn't going to prove such a great idea after all. He hadn't faced a woman before he'd shaved since Kate, and he wasn't sure he was up to it now.

"The early bird gets the worm, huh?" When he saw tell-tale splotches of color appear on her cheeks, he realized his words sounded sharper than he'd intended.

Despite her embarrassment, B.J.'s voice was crisp and cool when she answered. "The shower actually. in case there wasn't much hot water." To take the edge off her remark, B.J. added, "I think I left enough for you." The truth was she had awakened long before dawn, too apprehensive about her new job to sleep, but she wasn't going to admit that.

"No problem. I like 'em cold." *Especially when there's a need to keep cool*, he added silently. He reached for the coffee and took a hefty slug. "I suppose you've had breakfast, too?"

B.J. nodded, stifling the urge to offer to make breakfast for him while he showered. It was amazing how quickly a woman could be sucked into the nurturing role at the sight of a sleep-dazed man.

Grabbing his mug, Dana headed toward the bathroom. "Give me twenty minutes, and we'll be on our way."

B.J. made a sandwich and put it in her backpack, then added a piece of fruit and a can of juice. She was just closing the flap when Dana emerged from his shower and joined her at the counter.

He smelled of soap, shaving lotion, and clean laundry. At the fresh, manly scent of him, she took a quick breath and let it out slowly. What was there about a scrubbed male that made a woman's heart turn to mush? B.J. gave herself a mental shake and moved out of the range of temptation. She faced enough problems on this assignment without adding

Dana Thomas to her list. The guy was a hunk, she'd give him that, but she was through with men. Besides, it was obvious he was single by choice. By his own admission, he wasn't looking for anyone either. Then why was she getting vibes every time she was anywhere near him? *It must be the tropical heat*, she mused.

Dana threw a package of cheese and cracker sandwiches and a can of Coke into his battered briefcase then picked up the car keys. He stopped, keys poised in midair and gave her a questioning look. "My turn?"

"Right." Her hands felt clammy, and she was relieved at not having to deal with driving on the wrong side of a road this morning. Of course the other guys would probably think that Dana, as the superior male half of the arrangement, had been placed in charge of transportation. Well, she would enlighten them on that later. Right now, she had to concentrate on proving her worth as an operator and somehow she got the feeling that wasn't going to be easy.

Dana watched from the corner of his eye as the woman beside him wiped her palms unobtrusively on her jeans for the umpteenth time. He resisted the urge to reach out and pat her hand, to assure her it was going to be okay. Fact was, he wasn't at all sure it would be. He'd never worked with a woman operator before, and he suspected none of the other men had either. There was bound to be some mistrust of the unknown factor of a woman in a work place normally reserved for men. He wondered what had led her to choose this kind of job, and what she had done before this new assignment. She had admitted this was her first job out of the States, and for all their sakes, he hoped she could handle it.

The concrete block building of the chemical processing plant was almost dwarfed by the towering oil refinery beside it. As Dana drove into the parking lot, the four other men were just piling out of their cars. He braced himself for the innuendoes he expected, and they didn't disappoint him.

"Morning, Thomas," Frank Kelly drawled in his unmistakable Texas accent. "Get lots of sleep?" The emphasis was on *sleep*, and his eyes raked first Dana, then B.J. with a meaningful leer.

"Enough," Dana answered in a noncommittal tone.

"And how about you, Ms. Sutherland?" Frank gave an exaggerated bow in B.J.'s direction and studied her with avid interest.

"Just call me Sutherland, please," B.J. answered crisply and walked determinedly toward the door, ignoring his question.

Four pairs of eyes followed every unconscious sway of her trim backside while Dana pretended indifference.

"Let me know any time you want to trade places, Thomas," Pete Marshall said in a low voice as they fell in step behind her.

"You had your chance, Marshall," Dana said flatly and wondered why he felt angry at the avid interest his housemate had elicited from their fellow employees.

Albert Zurow was waiting inside the air-conditioned administration building and ushered the group into a small office. He offered the room's only chair to B.J., but she shook her head and took a step backward as though she was afraid he would insist on seating her. Zurow shrugged and sat down. "Sorry for the lack of space here. This won't take long. I trust you found your housing accommodations satisfactory?"

Dana saw Kelly and Marshall exchange sly grins at the question as the group nodded en masse. For B.J's sake, he was glad he'd volunteered himself. She would have had to lock herself in her room to be safe from either of those two.

After a moment, Zurow continued. "I assume all of you have read your assignment letter but just for the record, let me repeat. ChemCorp processes boron for use in smeltering aluminum and increased market prices have created a need for greater production. To facilitate that, we are bringing back into service a boiler that was mothballed about five years ago. I'm one of the few men still here who operated it prior to that time."

He paused and looked at the group crowded around him. "Today we'll begin with a walk-through to familiarize you with the overall project. Then I'll assign you each a locker and work space. I'll distribute prints and technical information for you to study. The break-in period should take a couple of weeks, and then you'll be ready to carry a shift and begin training the island personnel who will operate the equipment."

A couple of weeks? B.J. groaned silently. Why hadn't she realized it would take that long before she and Dana Thomas could go their separate ways? Two weeks seemed like forever. They'd be eating together, buying groceries together, sleeping together. Well, not in the usual meaning of the word, she hastily amended and felt heat rise from the base of her neck to her cheeks. What had she gotten herself into? She squared her shoulders and made a concerted effort to follow Albert Zurow's words.

After a brief look at the administrative building, they went outside to the boiler area. B.J.'s first job assignment had been in Minnesota and seeing part of the plant equipment in the open was a surprising new concept. They finished the walk-through before noon even with all the stops in which Albert Zurow introduced the new operators to various plant personnel. To say that the presence of B.J. in the small entourage attracted attention would be a gross understatement. Every man from janitor to plant manager stopped working to gawk. But if B.J. was aware of the sensation she was creating, she covered it with the aplomb of a Broadway actress.

Their final stop was the welcome cool inside the building that contained the control room and its small but well-equipped adjacent kitchen. Albert Zurow motioned toward a closed door at one end. "We'll take a break here, men." He glanced at B.J. and quickly added, "Uh, people."

"Would you care to use the powder room first, Ms. Sutherland?" Frank Kelly asked in a magnanimous voice.

"After you, Mister Kelly," B.J. answered in a clear voice.

Looking flustered, Frank Kelly sauntered toward the facility. When he emerged, he made a point of checking his zipper while Dana did a slow burn.

Pretending not to notice, B.J. took her turn, the only evidence of her discomfort the high color in her cheeks when she emerged.

Dana supposed the woman had encountered this kind of thing before but that didn't keep him from wanting to mash the smirk off several faces that watched her. This feeling of protectiveness was new to him, and he wasn't pleased with it. Since Kate there had been only himself, and he planned to keep it that way. Caring caused hurt, and he'd had his share of that for a lifetime. In the real world it was every man for himself. That went for every woman, too. Taking his own turn, Dana vowed not to forget it.

For the fifth night in a row, Dana showered after work then dressed in slacks and a sport shirt to go out with the other men for drinks and dinner. It wasn't that he wanted to leave the villa every evening. In fact, nothing would have pleased him more than to heat a microwave dinner, kick back, watch TV for a while, and then take a look at the never-ending prints Zurow kept handing out. Still, he felt his house-mate deserved a couple of hours alone to do whatever she did to make herself look so good.

"Need anything while I'm out?" he asked as he reached for the keys on the kitchen counter. The words had a familiar ring. He had asked the question often of Kate.

"No thanks."

She was slicing a carrot with the precision of a surgeon doing a routine operation and didn't look up. A cucumber, celery stalk, and radishes lay on the cutting board awaiting the knife. Chunks of lettuce and tomato wedges already filled a large salad bowl. It was a domestic scene he had witnessed many times. Only the woman was not the same.

"Don't you ever eat anything but rabbit food?" he asked in an effort to break his nostalgic thoughts before they turned maudlin. "Something filling, I mean."

"Like greasy burgers, fries, and beer?" She smiled disarmingly, and he wished she'd do it more often. B.J. Sutherland wore her strictly-business expression as consistently as she wore her Levis.

He hadn't seen her without either at the plant and hadn't much at the villa either. He had taken his cue from her and stayed fully clothed after that first morning when he'd stumbled into the kitchen in the sweat shorts he'd slept in. B.J. hadn't seemed pleased at his state of undress, and he couldn't exactly blame her. They were strangers living together under the same roof. He understood her need for privacy and respect toward one another. Since that morning, he made an effort to throw a shirt and pants on in the morning, if only to keep it from becoming an issue. "Touche" He grinned good-naturedly. "See you later."

Less than an hour had passed when Dana slowed the Escort for the curve leading to Schooner Bay. After a couple of beers, Pete Marshall had suggested driving to the Buccaneer Hotel for dinner and calypso music since it was Friday night, and they had the weekend off. It would have been too crowded with five men in one small car, so he used that excuse to bow out and head home. A Saturday morning hangover held no appeal for him, and he was reluctant to leave B.J. alone in the villa for hours with no idea of where he was. He could have called her, of course, but not without the risk of making a fool of himself. As it was, he'd had to ignore Frank Kelly's remark about *going home to his little housefrau* and the laughter it brought from the others.

Dana parked the car and unlocked the iron gate, noting B.J.'s room was dark. It was too early for her to be asleep, so that meant she was somewhere else in the house, probably enjoying her few hours of solitude. He hoped he wouldn't disturb her when he rummaged in the kitchen for something to eat. Belatedly, he wished he'd gotten a carry-out or had something at the bar.

When he entered the kitchen, B.J. was sitting at the dining table, her shoulders hunched over a set of prints. She jerked around at the sound of him entering the room, almost overturning the light-weight bamboo chair as she stood to face him. "What are you doing here?" she asked in a sharp voice.

He reacted to her tone with a flash of anger. "I live here, in case you've forgotten." Despite his annoyance, Dana couldn't stop his eyes from straying to the rest of her body.

She was wearing a short terry cloth wrap-around which exposed several inches of her shapely thighs. His appraising glance wasn't lost on her and telltale color flushed her face.

"But I thought you'd be—"

"Is there a rule against coming home early?" he demanded.

"No, of course not." She tugged at her robe and took a step toward the bedrooms. "I just didn't expect...so I didn't dress again..."

Dana's anger dissipated when he realized the reason for her harsh reaction to his arrival. Clearly he had embarrassed the woman, coming back and surprising her this way. He found her modesty oddly appealing, and her embarrassment out of character with her no nonsense attitude. Maybe they ought to talk about being a little more casual around the villa, but he'd deal with that later.

"You're pretty well covered as far as I can see." He turned away and headed for the kitchen as she made her escape.

Dana checked the contents of his section of the refrigerator and found nothing more appealing than a package of lunch meat. Slapping half of it between two slices of rye bread, he grabbed a can of Coke and sat down to devour it. Suddenly B.J. streaked through the room toward the veranda, and he caught a glimpse of scarlet lace and satin underthings before she whisked them out of sight and sprinted back to her bedroom.

Chewing more slowly, Dana grinned to himself, savoring this new bit of knowledge about his enigmatic house-mate. So the prim and proper Miss Sutherland wasn't just one of the boys after all. Under her starched white shirt and Levis, she had been wearing that red-hot underwear all day. Frank Kelly's eyeballs would have popped out of his head if he'd known. For that matter, eyeballs would have been popping all over the plant, even his. Dana put down his sandwich. Now that he knew about her sensual delicates, he wondered how he was ever going to look at B.J. Sutherland again without imagining her next-to-naked in something red and racy. It was going to be distracting to say the least.

B.J. had her back pressed against her closed bedroom

door, clutching the offending garments to her chest in horror. She had just behaved like some innocent Victorian maiden, dashing back to the veranda to retrieve her damp lingerie. Why had she panicked when she thought her house-mate might catch a glimpse of her laundry? Because it was cranberry froth, that's why. They were certainly not the standard underwear for IPPS operators. It was the one indulgence she allowed herself to appease her femininity in a man's world. She'd never intended for any of her co-workers to see them, thus throwing her right back into the category of invading woman. Even worse, Dana Thomas might interpret her wearing red undies as an invitation issued by a siren.

Well, she would just have to show him differently. B.J. flung the clothing onto the unused bed, changed into something more appropriate, tucked in her shirt, and forced herself to return to the dining room.

Dana was leaning over her abandoned prints and didn't seem to hear B.J. approach until she spoke.

"Are you familiar with this Bailey feedwater controls system?" she asked in a brisk voice.

He turned quickly, keeping his expression neutral. "I've worked with one like it before."

She pulled a chair up beside him. "Then how about explaining the three element drum level control to me? I got kind of lost on it."

Dana's arm brushed hers as he angled the binder so B.J. could have a better view. Her skin was soft and warm. She smelled faintly of vanilla and herbal shampoo, causing him to inhale her feminine scent with nostalgic longing for a moment. He edged far enough away from her to avoid further accidental contact, aware that she was doing the same thing while trying to appear totally engrossed in the print before her. So she wasn't immune to his touch, he thought with satisfaction before cautioning himself that this made it even more risky to be living with the woman. He took a deep, steadying breath. "First, do you understand that you have to have three input signals?"

"You mean drum level, feedwater flow and steam flow?" she asked quickly.

"You've got it. I'd say you've done your homework." He looked at her with interest and asked the question that had been on his mind all week. "What made you become an operator, B.J.?"

She hesitated as if weighing how much she wanted to tell him before she answered. "Oh, I knew someone who went through the program. It seemed like something I could learn to do." She shrugged. "The money is good, and I like to travel."

"And you enjoy the challenge of doing a man's job?"

"I like proving I can do the job as well as a man, yes," she answered decisively. "I've already told you, but I feel the need to once again point out that I'm not looking..." She let the words trail off.

"For a man?" he finished, making it sound like a question.

"No way," B.J. spat out the words, leaving no doubt of her feelings on the subject. She flipped another page over. "Now could we take a look at this last print?"

Dana obliged her, focusing on the details of the system before them, but his thoughts were still on her answer. So she had known someone in the IPPS program, a man of course. Was he the one who had caused her to swear off men? Was it that man she had to prove something to? He gave himself a mental shake. It was absolutely none of his business, and he didn't intend to make it any. He'd done the woman a favor, and they were managing the situation just fine so far. No need to complicate things by getting too friendly even if she were willing. Better to keep his distance, in every way possible.

They continued to discuss the boiler feedwater system as Dana answered all of B.J.'s discerning questions.

Then she pushed back her chair and stood. "Thanks for your help." She gave him a grateful smile.

"Actually, I should be thanking you." Dana also stood. "Reviewing this material orally is helpful to me, too." He hesitated as an idea formed in his mind, then impulsively acted upon it. "We could study the prints together every evening next week if you like."

"But you go out to din—"she began.

"I'd just as soon not. That is, unless you want time—"

Now it was she who interrupted, as the reason for his evening absences dawned on her. "You don't have to leave on my account. As you reminded me earlier, you live here, too."

"But I thought you might like some privacy and—"

"Look, Thomas," she was all business-like now, "I thought

we'd already established that I want no concessions made on my behalf. I don't need space any more than you do."

"Okay, but if I hang around, you've got to stop being so uptight about formal dress."

"Formal dress?" She looked puzzled, then nodded. "Oh, you mean like wearing my robe?"

"Yeah, or shorts or whatever. Couldn't we relax the dress code a little?"

She hesitated a moment. "I suppose so."

"Fine. And I understand from the other guys that there's a pool for our use here. Did you bring a swim suit?" When she nodded, he went on, "Then we'll have a swim some evening."

"I don't know," she began slowly.

"You can swim, can't you, Sutherland?"

"Yes, I can swim," she admitted reluctantly. "That sounds like fun." She turned toward the bedrooms. "See you in the morning."

Her scent remained behind her in the slight breeze stirred by the paddles from the overhead fan. Dana closed his eyes and breathed deeply. In spite of her efforts to be one of the guys, B.J. Sutherland was all female. He shook his head and in an effort to break the spell, stepped out onto the veranda. He looked toward the dark water below, his mind full of turmoil. Palm fronds brushed the screen like gentle whispers and a night bird called to its mate. What had he gotten himself into? Studying with his house-mate every evening, lounging around in casual clothes, even taking a dip in the pool. It was beginning to sound more like a marriage than a housing arrangement. His mouth seemed to say things his head didn't agree with, but it wasn't like the situation was going to be long-term. In a week they'd be on opposite shifts, and the job would likely end in a couple of months. Then they'd probably never see each other again. Or at least never live together again.

The woman was smart and obviously eager to learn. She'd made a good impression on this assignment. It wouldn't hurt him to share a little of his knowledge and experience with her. He smiled inwardly. He'd do the same for any guy, even if he didn't wear red underwear.

CHAPTER THREE

B.J. opened the bi-fold louvered doors to the alcove that separated the washer and dryer from the kitchen proper. Emptying her laundry bag on top of the dryer, she set controls, then measured soap powder as the washing machine filled. She hadn't slept well and had awakened with vivid dreams of Dana Thomas still in her mind. She blushed remembering those intimate images. It must be sharing close quarters with a man again, creating a situation not unlike her marriage.

She had resisted the impulse to reach for her Levis this morning and dressed in tailored white shorts and a yellow tee shirt instead. She had to admit, the casual attire was much cooler and more comfortable.

"Do you always get up so early on your days off?" Dana grumbled as he appeared in the kitchen.

"Absolutely." She dumped the powder into the swirling water and watched for a few minutes, forcing herself to concentrate on the soapsuds instead of the appealing, unkempt man behind her.

"Will you teach me how to do laundry?" he asked suddenly.

She turned to face him, surprised to find that he was serious. "You don't know how to do laundry?"

"Not really. I just dump dirty clothes in a machine, add a random amount of soap, and hope for the best. I'd like to know the proper way to do it, with the clothes sorted as they should be and such. You see, my wife always did it before—

"He stopped at her shocked expression, realizing what he'd just said.

"I thought you weren't married." She lifted an eyebrow and waited.

Dana turned red. He hadn't meant to tell her about Kate. "I'm not." He clamped his mouth shut as he met her accusing stare. Ex-wife would be inaccurate, and he couldn't bear to say late wife.

"Oh," she said in the silence that followed, and sensing that the subject was closed, made an effort to lessen the tension that was almost palpable in the small laundry area.

B.J. picked up a wrinkled sheet. "You separate the clothes first, whites and very light-colored things together, then darks together. For whites you can use hot water or warm. Cold is best for darks. Next you fill the tub with water of proper temperature . . ." As B.J. continued to give a lesson in laundry, her mind was busy trying to assimilate the new information she had just acquired. Dana Thomas was divorced. She should have known a man like him would be. Or maybe he wasn't? She doubted if her ex-husband had confessed he was a married man before having the affair that led to the end of their ten year marriage.

What was this man's game? Pretend to be single and play house with the female operator? It was a good thing for her he'd been caught in the web of his own lie...if it was a lie. Since there was no way she could be sure, she would just have to assume the worst. It only proved once again that she couldn't trust men, not even in the work place.

They managed to get through a shared breakfast of coffee, fruit and croissants while doing laundry. Then Dana offered to run the sweeper while B.J. cleaned the kitchen and dusted. It was only for this one weekend, B.J. told herself. Then they'd be on shift work and the unwelcome togetherness would be over. By mid-morning, they faced a sparkling clean villa and a pile of freshly washed and folded laundry, with hours of free time left.

"You can take the car if you like," Dana offered halfheartedly.

"No, I should catch up on e-mail," B.J. countered without enthusiasm. "You go ahead."

"You surely don't want to waste this nice day on the island staring at a computer screen." Dana hesitated a moment, searching for a solution that would be equitable for both, then asked, "Do you play golf?"

"A little." B.J. thought of all those weekends she had spent on the golf course with Tom and wondered if his new wife had taken her place there, too.

"Then why don't we drive over to the Buccaneer and play a round?"

"If you like," B.J. said with little enthusiasm. It wasn't that she would rather answer e-mails than get out of the villa, but she would have preferred to go alone. She wasn't sure how she felt about Dana Thomas, and she needed time to sort it out. Spending days and nights with the guy for almost a week had made her aware of being a woman again. She didn't want to feel the kind of attraction for any man that she was feeling for him. He obviously had secrets, which meant she couldn't fully trust him. Being attracted to someone you didn't trust was a guaranteed recipe for disaster. She couldn't very well avoid him, so there was only one way to get the feeling out of her system. She would have to go along with him and be just one of the guys like he asked.

Dana drove the short distance to the hotel where they asked directions to the pro shop. Soon they were equipped with rented clubs and shoes.

B.J. was still wearing her white shorts, but she had put on a long white shirt over her yellow knit top and added a billed cap to match it. It was going to be difficult to concentrate on his game with a pair of legs like those to distract him, Dana admitted.

"Shall we share a cart?" he asked as they assembled their equipment.

"I'd prefer to walk," she answered. "Better exercise."

"Okay." She would be wise to save her energy for the game, he thought, but he'd have to let her find that out for herself. They could always ride the last nine if need be.

In summer season, the resort was not crowded and using pull carts was allowed, so they rented two, stashed their bags, and walked toward the first tee.

"Ladies first." Dana gestured toward the verdant manicured mound.

"No," B.J. shook her head, "let's flip for it."

"Whatever you say." Dana reached into his pocket for a quarter. "Your call." He slapped the coin on his palm, keeping it covered until she spoke.

"Heads."

He raised his hand. "Sorry. Tails." Still holding the quarter, he looked at her. "Want to play for a quarter a hole, just to make it a little more interesting?"

"Why not a dollar and make it really interesting?" she challenged.

Dana hesitated. He hated to take that much money away from her. "I usually shoot in the mid-eighties," he warned her.

"Fair warned is fair armed," she answered.

"You're on." He pulled out his driver and walked toward the tee. With the ball aligned, he hit a drive straight down the fairway.

"Nice shot," B.J. said with obvious sincerity.

"Thanks." Dana watched the ball roll to a stop about one hundred and fifty yards from the first green. He stepped back and waited for B.J. to take her shot.

She reached in her bag for her driver, bent to tee up her ball, and took a couple of practice swings. Perfect form, Dana observed, in every sense of the word. Now we'll see if she can hit the ball. He was so engrossed in watching how she swung her club and connected squarely with the ball that he forgot to take his eyes off her to track it. When he belatedly remembered to do so, he saw that her ball had landed at least fifteen yards beyond his own.

"Good shot," he admitted magnanimously.

"Thank you." Maybe it was just his imagination that her words were edged with a tinge of cautious gloating.

As they walked down the fairway with the sun at their backs and a magnificent view of the sparkling bright blue Caribbean in the distance, Dana felt a sense of euphoria at being alive. Then he thought of Kate and Jared, and the guilt for their senseless deaths settled on him with its familiar heavy weight. He had no right to be here, to be anywhere enjoying himself. Seeking to break the silence that left too much space for thinking, Dana asked, "So, do you play much golf?"

"I used to, but not in a while." Her voice sounded sad, but she didn't elaborate, and he didn't press it.

"Me, too."

"It's beautiful here, isn't it?" B.J. turned to him, and her eyes were the same color as the sea beyond.

"Is getting my mind on the scenery a diversion to throw me off my game?" She was beautiful and that was the real diversion he had to watch out for, Dana admitted to himself.

"None intended," she said and waited silently as he took an 8-iron from his bag and addressed the ball.

He swung, and the ball landed neatly on the green with a good chance for a birdie. He breathed easier.

"Nice shot," B.J. said automatically as she approached her own ball and analyzed its position. She selected a 9-iron and took a swing. The ball sailed easily over the one hundred and thirty five yards needed to land on the front of the green and rolled within a foot of the pin.

Dana gave a low whistle under his breath. Damn, she was good. Nobody had that kind of luck twice in a row. "Nice shot," he conceded as they pulled their carts toward the green. B.J. marked her ball and stepped back as Dana lined up his putt. With great concentration, he stroked the ball into the cup for a birdie. This was more like it. He could afford to be gracious now.

Gesturing toward the ball she had just placed back into position, he said, "Yours is good. Just pick it up."

"I'd rather putt," she insisted stubbornly and tapped it in the cup.

That's the last time I try to give her a putt, Dana fumed silently as he marked his scorecard. "So nobody wins this one. Want to play carryover?" By allowing the winner of a hole to take all scores tied previously, he knew he would have an edge, but at this point he felt like taking any advantage he could.

"Sure, why not?" She didn't look up as she entered her own score.

As they walked in silence toward the second tee, Dana knew that B.J. Sutherland was out for blood. A game of golf was just one more chance to play her personal game of one upmanship, so he would give her a run for her money and let the best man win.

Hole after hole they slugged it out as the sun climbed higher and the day grew hotter. Dana, in khaki shorts and shirt, was perspiring profusely while B.J. remained cool and composed. He had suggested they stop after the ninth hole and have lunch, hoping to get his second wind. He needed to gain back the lead he'd lost. Their series of ties had been broken on the fourth hole, giving him three carryover points. From that small victory on, it had been downhill all the way. He had hit one ball in the rough, lost one in the water, and hit two out of bounds.

B.J. had insisted on playing through, unwilling to break her concentration and precarious winning streak. As they made their way to the eighteenth hole, Dana was trailing by nine strokes and was psyching himself up to be a gracious loser.

Men don't like losing to a woman, B.J. reminded herself as she lined up her ball for a shot at the green, but she wasn't going to shoot less than her best just to appease any man. She'd often done that with Tom and look what it had gotten her. A no-fault divorce, that's what. She hit the ball with more force that necessary and it sailed over the green to land out of sight in the rough. B.J. took a deep breath as she replaced her club. That's what happened from picturing Tom Sutherland's face instead of the golf ball. She'd lost at least one point, but she had plenty to spare. Dana Thomas was looking positively wilted, and she had a momentary twinge of conscience for not accepting his suggestion to stop for lunch. Her need to prove that she could take the heat and keep on winning had gotten the better of her.

"Too bad," Dana said and tried to sound more sincere than he felt at the moment. It was obvious she was going to beat him by several strokes and anything that closed the distance between their scores was welcome.

He got off a nice shot and was in a good position to make another birdie as he approached the green. From the undergrowth at the edge of the course, he watched as B.J. hunted for her ball.

"Eeeiii," she suddenly shrieked and drew back in horror from something in the tall grass.

Dropping his club, he was beside her in a second. "What is it?" He pushed her behind him, then caught a glimpse of the small snake wriggling away, obviously more frightened than the woman who'd almost stepped on it.

"It's just a harmless little black snake, and he's making a fast getaway." She was still trembling, so he put an arm around her shoulders and grinned reassuringly. "It's nothing to be afraid of."

"If you say so." B.J. made an effort to pull herself together and look halfheartedly for her lost ball.

"Let it go," Dana told her. "Let's get out of this tangle of weeds and get on with the game." This time she didn't argue with him. So Miss Tough-Guy had an Achilles' heel, and he'd just found it, he thought with perverse amusement.

B.J. meekly took a one stroke penalty on the eighteenth, chipped, and putted out. Then Dana made his putt for another birdie, and they totaled up their scores.

"Eighty-five," he said as he folded his score card and dropped it in his shirt pocket.

"Seventy-nine," she told him with quiet pride.

He took out his billfold and counted eight one dollar bills and held them out.

She took the money. "Thanks. Winner buys lunch." When he started to protest, she waved it away. "Custom, Thomas."

"Okay, but I warm you, Sutherland, I'm starved."

"Then let's try The Terrace buffet we saw, so I don't have to spend much more than my winnings to feed you." She tucked the bills into the side pocket of her still crisply-creased shorts and headed toward the pro shop.

"Hey, hey, hey. Who have we here?" Frank Kelly was driving toward them, with Pete Marshall beside him in the cart as they left the green.

"So Miss Sutherland plays golf, too, eh Thomas?" Marshall spoke in Dana's direction but didn't take his eyes off B.J.

Dana didn't like Marshall's implication of what else B.J. might be doing but he decided to let it go. "And she's good at it."

"I'll just bet she is," Kelly gave a low, meaningful laugh, still looking at B.J.

"How good?" Marshall persisted.

Dana opened his mouth to answer, but B.J. beat him to it. "Not good enough to beat Thomas but I hung in there."

"Too bad we got a late start, too much rum last night." Kelly shook his head regretfully. "Maybe we can make it a foursome next Saturday?"

The question was directed at B.J., and she answered for both of them. "Maybe. I can't make plans this far ahead. Have a nice game, guys, and watch out for the snake on the eighteenth hole." She turned toward Dana. "Let's get going,

Thomas. I'm starved."

As they continued on toward the pro shop, Dana said shortly. "That wasn't necessary. You weren't obligated to try to salvage my male pride."

"I didn't do it for you, Thomas," she said flatly. "I did it for me. I didn't want to show my hand too soon, in case I feel like making any more bets."

She was either the world's best actress, or she was really serious about her intentions. Either way, he was glad she hadn't let those guys know she'd beaten him. He would never have heard the last of it. All in all, he wasn't too sorry about losing to her. She'd played a good game, a fair game, and asked no favors. A man had to admire a woman with her grit, even if it did stick in his craw from time to time.

CHAPTER FOUR

The Terrace was still crowded in mid-afternoon, Dana noticed, as he and B.J. waited to be seated. Probably assuming they were honeymooners, the maitre d' led them to a secluded table behind a fountain where they had a good view of each other and nothing else. Not that he was complaining. The woman who sat opposite him was great to look at with her Caribbean-colored eyes and short-cropped hair that framed a fine featured face. The day's sun had heightened the color on her high cheek bones and humidity caused dampened wisps of her hair to form curly tendrils on her slender neck as she bent to study the menu.

A waiter came to take their order and B.J. spoke to Dana twice before he heard her. "I said, I'm having the buffet. Is that all right with you, too?"

"Yes, fine. And iced tea with lemon."

"Make that two." She gave her menu to the waiter. "And I'll take the check, please."

"Yes, madam."

Damnation. There had been no call for that. Now the smug waiter would assume he was some kind of gigolo.

"What are you looking so grim about, Thomas? Haven't you ever had a woman pick up a check before?" B.J. asked as soon as the waiter was out of earshot.

"I don't think I have, now that you mention it." He was glad they were behind the fountain where the other diners wouldn't be able to observe the humiliating situation.

"There's no reason to be embarrassed by this," she continued. "It's part of the equal opportunity thing."

"I suppose you do this with all the men you go out with?"

"Only when I beat them at golf." She gave him a rueful smile. "Actually, I don't go out with men."

Uh-oh. This possibility hadn't entered his mind. "Then you prefer ..." he began tentatively.

"Oh no, never. Is that what you thought I meant?" She looked horrified. "Just because I do the work of a man, it doesn't mean..." She took a slow breath, then blew it out. "Let's get this straight just for the record, Thomas. I don't go out with men, because men have a way of complicating your life. And I don't want to complicate my life anymore."

He frowned. "What did you mean by that?"

"Oh." Momentarily flustered that she had told him something she hadn't intended, she floundered. "I just meant... well, any more than it already is, that's all."

She was saved from further explanations when the waiter returned with their drinks and invited them to partake of the buffet.

Following B.J. to the long tables laden with a colorful display of exotic dishes, Dana wondered what she had really meant about complications in her life. It must have something to do with the guy she knew in IPPS. Had she been married to him? Not likely. He had probably turned her down, possibly after an affair. Maybe he hadn't liked her picking up the check either.

They dined on shrimp, lobster, and chicken accompanied by salads and fresh vegetables. After they sated themselves, they talked. Dana, feeling an obligation to fulfill his role of dinner guest, entertained his hostess with tales of his IPPS travels. He was careful to omit locations that had included Kate and Jared, which wasn't difficult since he'd done start-up and testing for thirteen years and been married less than five of those. They ordered strong, black coffee and returned to the buffet to sample the sinful array of tropical fruits and dessert.

Mid-afternoon turned to early evening as they lingered on the stone terrace of the hotel, lulled by the trickling water of the fountain and the fragrance of tropical blooms that spilled over the wrought-iron railing beside their table. It was the nearest thing to a date that Dana had experienced in the two years since he'd been alone, and he had forgotten how enjoyable the company of an attractive woman could be. Even one determined to be just another guy.

B.J. sipped her coffee slowly, reluctant to end the magic afternoon. She had told Dana Thomas the truth; she never went out with men although she hadn't lacked opportunities. It was pleasant to sit and talk with an interesting male, laugh at his escapades, and feel his eyes on her in silent admiration. She hadn't experienced any of these things in almost four years. *There was a good reason for that*, she reminded herself sternly. Going out with a man could lead to caring, and caring led to getting hurt. She had vowed that she would never leave herself open for heartbreak again. Yet here she was, dangerously close to letting her guard down, and with a man who could have a wife back home for all she knew. She placed her credit card on the tray with the check and motioned for the waiter.

"I'll get the tip." Dana reached once again for his well-worn billfold.

"I plan to add it to my charge." B.J. pulled the tray towards her.

"If you are paying for lunch, I can at least pick up the tip," Dana said with finality as he threw a bill almost as large as the check beside her card.

The battle of wills was decided by the waiter who scooped up the tray before B.J. could remove the money.

"Thank you," she said, then added testily, "but it wasn't necessary."

"I thought it was," Dana shot back. "To appease my masculine pride, I suppose."

"Well put." She pushed back her chair as she saw the waiter coming, not waiting for Dana to do the honor.

"Back to being just one of the guys, huh?" he asked wryly as he stood.

"I've never tried to be anything else, Thomas," she said firmly as they left The Terrace.

"Have it your way, Sutherland," he conceded as he walked faster to keep up with her, "but for a moment there, I almost thought you were a woman."

B.J. didn't bother to answer his facetious remark. She'd succeeded in doing what she meant to do. The hypnotizing glow of the afternoon had evaporated, and they were bickering like normal, but a small part of her wished that they weren't.

The heat of the day didn't dissipate with the coming of darkness, and the ceiling fans in the villa were ineffective against it. B.J. went to her room to work on her laptop computer, but she was unable to concentrate and soon gave it up.

Dana watched golf on television but the oppressive heat made him too restless to sit still, so he switched the set off and wandered out onto the veranda. He considered going out but nightlife held no appeal for him, and he decided against it.

B.J. came into the kitchen for something to drink. She had showered and dressed in a pale blue one-piece outfit that he could only describe as a sort of romper suit. Whatever it was, it looked good on her, he grudgingly admitted.

It wasn't enough that she had beat him at golf. She'd added insult to injury by picking up the check for lunch and made a big deal over him getting the tip. She was calling all the shots here. Maybe it was time he showed her that she wasn't really one of the guys after all. "I was just thinking of making a pitcher of pina coladas. Would you like one?" he asked as he joined her.

"Okay." She moved to the counter and sat down to watch.

Dana removed pineapple juice and bottles of light and dark rum from the cabinet. He placed a pitcher on the counter beside the blender and took a tray of ice cubes from the freezer. In a few minutes, he had mixed and filled a tall pitcher and poured two drinks, giving one to B.J.

She took a sip of her drink and nodded. "Delicious."

"Thank you." He sampled his own drink. "Cruzan Rum is hard to beat anywhere." The air in the villa seemed suddenly more stifling. "It's hot in here." He toyed with his glass, then said casually. "What would you think of taking this pitcher to the pool and finishing our drinks out there?"

B.J. gave the question serious thought. She knew where this could lead, but then, it could be just a drink at the pool as he had said if that was what she wanted it to be. It was hot in the villa, and she was tempted. "Okay, sounds good to me."

"Five minutes to put your swimsuit on," he said as he set

his glass on the counter.

"But I thought we were just..."

"Nobody goes to the pool unprepared to swim." He looked at her and grinned. "Unless they want to risk getting their clothes wet." He looked at his watch. "Five minutes and counting."

B.J. gave him a suspicious look before climbing to her feet and making her way into her bedroom. She leaned against her closed bedroom door, biting her lip thoughtfully. She would wear a cover-up over her swimsuit. She wouldn't be any more exposed than she was now, though it wasn't her body she hesitated to expose to Dana Thomas' discerning eyes. It was the feelings that she couldn't seem to control when she was near him. She'd kept her emotions bottled up for such a long time. Now they threatened to escape and run amok, and she seemed powerless to stop them. *It's only a swim*, she told herself firmly. *Nothing else*. With those encouraging words, she exited her bedroom to join Dana once again.

"One minute to spare." Dana held up his arm and tapped a finger on the face of his watch as B.J. reappeared in the kitchen doorway. "You've probably set a record here."

B.J. stopped and stared at the man who stood before her. The sight of his lean, deeply-tanned body accented his dark good looks, literally taking her breath away. Her eyes followed the tangle of dark hair covering his muscular chest to the place where it disappeared at the line of his black, fitted trunks. Lust was an unfamiliar emotion for her, and lust was all that she could be feeling right now, because she scarcely knew Dana Thomas. What she knew of him led her to believe that he couldn't be trusted any more than her ex-husband. That thought turned the liquid fire in her veins to ice water quite effectively, and she picked up her drink from the counter. "Let's go," she said in a voice that sounded almost normal.

Dana held the door open, and B.J. walked through, taking care not to brush against him in the narrow foyer. She hadn't brought her house keys, so she was obliged to wait at the iron gate until he unlocked it and held aside an overhanging bougainvillea branch for her to pass.

"The pool is over the next hill. Want to walk?" he asked.

"Fine."

She matched his steps easily and behind them a full

moon cast their elongated shadows on the asphalt road as they walked. The night was silent except for the tinkling of ice in their glasses and the pitcher Dana carried, synchronized with the muted slapping of their thong sandals on the pavement. The warm air was fragrant with the perfume of oleanders that lined their path.

The pool was dark except for underwater lighting that gave the water an eerie glow. Dana placed the pitcher on a small table and motioned toward the lounge chairs on either side. "Let's finish our drinks, shall we?"

B.J. sank gratefully onto the chaise and sipped her drink in silence, allowing the ambience of the tropical paradise to calm her turbulent emotions. When Dana proffered the pitcher, she held out her glass for more. She seldom drank alcohol and the rum-laced concoction left a very pleasant afterglow deep inside.

Dana swirled the ice in his glass and studied it. "Mind if I ask you something?"

"Will you ask anyway?" she responded lightly.

"Probably." He grinned. "What's your name?"

"B.J. Sutherland." She giggled. "And you are?"

"No, your real name. What do the initials stand for?"

"Promise you'll never tell anyone?" She had worked hard to change her image from a housewife to an operator, and she guarded her new persona with serious intent.

"Promise."

"Betty Jo."

"Betty Jo Sutherland," Dana said softly. "It fits you."

"No it doesn't," she denied. "Not anymore."

Idly, he wondered if the man in her past had led her to deny the attractive female she really was. B.J. might suit the IPPS operator best, but tonight she was Betty Jo. She was all woman, and he was going to prove it to her.

When they had drained the pitcher, Dana stood. "Come on, let's try the water."

B.J. rose and moved in slow motion to the pool's edge.

"I think you'd better take your robe off first," Dana said as he moved to stand behind her. "Here, let me help."

His hands brushed her bare skin as he took the garment from her shoulders, and she shivered at the contact.

"Cold?" he asked softly, and she shook her head. He took her hand and led her down the steps into the water.

She wore a plain maillot as he had expected but the un-relieved style outlined every perfect curve of her well-proportioned body. The suit was a shade of blue that shone silver in the underwater lights, and he was reminded of an exotic tropical fish ...or a mermaid. Desire shot through his body like a bolt of lightning, and his voice was husky when he spoke. "Come on, let's explore the deep." He swam slowly toward the other side of the pool, matching his powerful strokes to hers.

She swam gracefully, as she did everything else. And he was constantly aware of her femininity in spite of all her ef-forts to conceal it behind her mask of bravado.

When they reached the deep end, he dived below the surface and pulled her down with him. He then placed his hands on her small waist and brought her up again.

"No fair," she spluttered. "I wasn't expecting that."

"Swimming isn't fun for a guy if he can't dunk someone."

"That's too juvenile to merit a response, Thomas."

He rolled onto his back and gazed at the star-studded sky. "What a view."

She turned and floated beside him, her eyes scanning the heavens. "Looks almost close enough to touch," she said softly.

"I'd rather touch you." He reached out and took her arm. He pulled her into a vertical position, holding her away from his body by sheer willpower. He turned her to face the same direction as he and then whispered softly, "Look. The full moon above and the lights of Christiansted below. It's en-chantment."

She moved back against him as she looked skyward, and he felt a rush of desire. Turning her toward him, he pulled her into his arms and buried his face in her hair. Her arms slid around his neck, and he raised his eyes to meet hers. He was pleased to find a mirror image of what he felt.

Slowly, he bent his face until his lips were almost touch-ing hers. He stopped as if he would pull back from the brink of temptation, then surrendered and crushed her mouth in a searing kiss that seemed to go on forever. The flavor of fruit juice and rum left a lingering sweetness on her tongue, and he lost himself in the sensation.

It was a moment before either of them heard the car door slam in the parking area just below the pool.

He swore silently and gently pushed her away from him, holding her while she caught her balance. "We've got company."

She looked at him as if coming out of a dream, her eyes wide with apprehension. "I—I think we should go."

Half stumbling, she splashed through the water and climbed the steps. By the time he followed, she had already pulled on her robe and was waiting. They met the two strangers as they left the pool area, and Dana breathed a sigh of relief. For a moment, he had feared that it might be some of the guys from IPPS, and he had read that fear in B.J.'s eyes, too.

Saved, he said silently. Whether he meant from discovery or the woman beside him, he wasn't exactly certain. One thing was certain. He hadn't been in control of what was happening between them.

B.J. stood shivering as she waited for Dana to unlock the gate to the villa. She wasn't sure if it was from the night air on her wet body or the knowledge that she had almost lost control of her emotions back there in the pool and surrendered to the need that overwhelmed her when Dana Thomas kissed her. No, she'd have to face the truth. She had lost control and only the fortunate intervention of strangers had saved her from doing something utterly stupid. Her body, heedless of common sense, still churned with confused emotions.

Dana was taking a long time to open the gate, and once inside the patio, he fumbled again with the door lock while she waited impatiently. His behavior almost convinced her that he was as unnerved as she but that couldn't be. To him it had surely been a game of seduction, nothing more. If they'd been interrupted by the other men from IPPS, he would have probably felt a sense of male pride at being caught making out with the only female in the group. Men were like that, weren't they? What a disaster that would have been for her. She must have been out of her mind to allow a thing like that to happen in a public pool. Allow? She had practically invited it!

She swept past Dana as he opened the door and went directly to her room to change. She had to discuss what had happened with the man involved and the sooner the better, but she wanted them both to be fully clothed when she did so.

Coming into the living room a few minutes later, she was

relieved to see that her house-mate was wearing khakis and a tee shirt which covered the distracting parts of his attractive anatomy. She took a seat facing the sofa where he sat.

"We need to talk." She spoke in a clipped no-nonsense tone, and he looked up in surprise, then flicked off the TV.

"Okay."

"We almost made a big mistake a few minutes ago."

"Did we?" His eyes met hers and held them. "You seemed in agreement, unless I misunderstood your signals."

"I'd had three drinks. I wasn't thinking clearly."

"So that's the spin you're putting on it?" He shook his head in disbelief even as he secretly acknowledged the truth of her accusation. "I plied you with liquor and then tried to seduce you?"

"I'm not placing blame. I just want to put this in the proper perspective."

"By all means," he agreed solemnly.

"Maybe it's of no consequence to you, but I have a reputation to consider. I don't want to be known as a woman who will sleep with every—"

"Wait a minute. It is of consequence to me, B.J. I don't go around sleeping with every woman I meet either." He hadn't planned to let this go that far. He stood up, jammed his hands in his pockets, walked toward the veranda, and then turned to face her. It was time to admit the truth. "I hadn't intended for this thing between us to get out of hand, but I felt something special for you, something I haven't felt for a woman in a long time. I thought you felt it, too."

He waited, and she finally said in a small voice, "Okay, I did feel it. We do seem to have a strong attraction toward each other, but that doesn't mean we have to act on it. I don't want to be involved with anyone. I thought I made that clear."

"Perfectly. And I felt the same way, but you seem to have changed all that. Now what I want is you."

He stood looking at her with such open desire on his handsome face that her breath caught in her throat. It would be so easy to get up and walk into his arms and continue what they had started in the pool.

"Get over it, Thomas. Just what part of no don't you understand?" Her voice was as brittle as glass, and she felt that she would shatter into a million pieces if he didn't stop looking at her with such longing. "I came here to do a job, same as you. It's important to my career to do it well. I couldn't afford to be involved with you even if I wanted to be. And I don't want to be."

"Don't you?"

He seemed determined not to let it go, but she was just as determined to put it to rest once and for all. "No." His dark eyes held hers still, demanding the truth. "Well, yes, but I'm not going to be. I've done that, and I won't do it ever again."

Too agitated to sit still any longer, she also stood and walked to the kitchen, putting the counter between them. "It's sharing this villa. We've been playing house, almost like being married and—"

"What do you know about being married?" Dana cut in. "I thought you said you'd been involved with—"

"Isn't marriage being involved?" she demanded, not answering his question. "At least, it is supposed to involve two people, isn't it?" When he didn't answer, she went on. "This is only for another week. Then we'll scarcely see each other. We're adults, Thomas."

"Yeah, that seems to be part of the problem, doesn't it?"

"You know what I mean. We can put this incident behind us and pretend it never happened." Her resolve was running out. She felt herself near tears and was at a loss to understand why.

Dana took a step toward her. "For what it's worth, I'd like to say I'm sorry. I acted on feeling tonight, but I have never forced myself on a woman, and I won't begin now."

His contrite apology sounded sincere, and she felt a tear roll down her cheek. She swiped it away with the back of her hand. "You were no more to blame than I. Let's just leave it that way and call a truce." She came around the counter and held out her hand. "Just friends?"

Instead of shaking it as she had intended, Dana took it and brought it to his lips and kissed her open palm.

Jerking her hand away, B.J. turned and fled to her room. After all her sensible rationalization, with one gesture he managed to reduce her to tears of frustration and regret. Closing the door, she threw herself onto her bed and bawled. There was no justice in the world. If there had been, she would have met Dana Thomas instead of Tom Sutherland, but now both their lives were too complicated with whatever the past had done to them, no matter how much either of them wished otherwise.

Remembering the pitcher and glasses, Dana returned to the pool. The people who had interrupted them earlier had gone now, and he sat down in the chaise to reconstruct what had happened between him and Betty Jo Sutherland. He had lost control of the situation when he'd touched her. It still scared him to realize how that happened. Like her, he had sworn not to get involved with anyone again. It wasn't worth the risk of being hurt, It was obvious she knew about hurting, too. Maybe she had been married to the guy with IPPS. She hadn't denied it. Either way, somebody had stomped on her heart big time. He was at a loss to understand why anybody would want to do that to her. Sure, she had that facade of bravado, but she was trying to make it in a man's world so she couldn't afford to be soft and feminine like Kate.

The thought of his wife brought the feeling of guilt that always accompanied it, only this time there was the added guilt of betrayal. He'd held another woman in his arms, kissed her, and wanted her. He'd sworn there would never be anyone else. That was to be his penance, and it was a small price to pay for what he'd caused. It was just as well that B.J. had rejected him, because he hadn't the will power to walk away from what he'd felt. He would abide by her decision, because he knew in his heart that it was the best thing for both of them.

CHAPTER
FIVE

B.J. welcomed the routine of Monday morning. She had spent most of Sunday in her room at the computer, determined to keep a safe distance from her house-mate.

He had slept late, then gone back to the pool, not asking her to join him. Finally in the late afternoon, he had gone out with the other men while she reviewed the feedwater prints again, but this time alone.

When their regular schedules started, she wouldn't have to work as hard to avoid Dana. She could keep the conversations light and impersonal. She would finish up this job and try to put all thoughts of him behind her. For now though, she would still have to have minimal interactions with him. "Care for a banana for lunch, Thomas?" she asked as Dana came into the kitchen. "These seem to be getting over-ripe."

"Sure, I'll take one." He took the fruit and set it aside to put in his lunch. They had both purchased insulated lunch boxes to protect their food from the heat.

B.J. finished filling hers and snapped the lid.

They drank their coffee in silence, because B.J. had learned quickly that Dana was not a morning person. Their personalities complimented each other. She drove the car mornings, because he didn't cope well with traffic snarls at that time of day, while he handled afternoon snafus better than she. But after this week, they'd each be on their own, she thought with a sense of relief, and she could concentrate fully on her work at the plant.

No mention was made of the weekend as they drove to

work . B.J. supposed Dana had taken her words to heart and the truce was working as she had hoped. As they parked, Frank Kelly and Pete Marshall pulled in beside them.

"Well, good morning, Miss Sutherland." Frank grinned broadly as he fell in step beside B.J. "You're looking bright and cheerful this morning. Have a good weekend?"

"It was okay." She kept her voice politely neutral.

"You should have come along with us last night. I'll bet you and I could have jived with the best to that calypso band."

"I don't dance," B.J. said.

"Don't dance?" He looked shocked. "Well, sweetheart, I can remedy that. Just wait till next weekend, and I'll teach you."

"Sorry, I'll have to study." B.J. bolted up the steps, leaving the men behind.

"My, my, she's touchy," Frank said to the other two. "Is she saving all her sweetness for you, Thomas?"

"What you see is what you get," Dana answered shortly.

B.J. put her lunch box in her locker then went into the conference room and unfolded her set of prints.

"Good morning, Miss Sutherland," Albert Zurow spoke from behind her.

She flinched at the sound of his voice. "Oh, good morning, Mister Zurow."

"Sorry I startled you. Is everything all right?"

"Yes, fine." Did he mean personally or with the job? But then, surely he couldn't know what a fiasco her weekend had been.

"Is the housing arrangement working out well?"

"Fine," she repeated, not meeting his eyes.

"I thought you looked a little—"

The other men came in just then and Zurow's words were left unfinished. A little what, she wondered uneasily.

When they broke for lunch , B.J. went to wash up first as was according to the established protocol. She had already taken her lunch box from her locker when the others joined her in the conference room where they ate. When she opened the lid, she bit her lip to stifle the scream that rose in her throat and clamped the lid down tight again. As unobtrusively as possible, she got up and left the room. Angry tears stung her eyes as she made her way outside and sat down on the steps. The sun was hot, but she didn't feel it. How could anyone be so low?

"Is something wrong?" It was Dana's voice behind her, but she didn't turn around.

"No, should there be?" She spat out the words.

"You didn't eat your lunch."

"No, I suddenly didn't have any appetite—for dead lizard."

"Dead liz—what the—"

"Don't bother to pretend you didn't put it there."

"Me? Why would I put a dead lizard in your lunch box?" He sounded sincerely shocked, but she wasn't buying it.

"I don't know. You tell me." She turned and glared at him.

"Listen, I don't pull juvenile pranks like that, and I can't understand why you think I had anything to do with it."

"Because you know how I hate creepy crawly things."

He frowned. "Oh, you mean the snake?"

"It was a rotten thing to do, Thomas. Just to get even."

"Get even?" His perplexity deepened. "For what? You don't think I'd stoop to this because you beat me at golf?" Another thought flashed in his mind. "Or because of what happened at the pool—"

"Miss Sutherland? Are you all right?" Albert Zurow asked from the doorway.

"I'm fine, Mister Zurow. Just a touch of stomach virus but it's better now."

She stood and passed Dana Thomas without another look.

He watched her go with mixed emotions. Somebody had tried to get to her, and he wished he knew who it was, but even as he understood her reasoning, he deeply resented her blaming him.

Just three more days, B.J. reminded herself with grim determination as she adjusted the straps of her backpack and joined her house-mate for the ride to work. Then their only contact would be at the plant when changing shifts and that would be strictly business. "My turn," she held out her hand for the keys Dana had already taken from the counter.

"Sorry," he mumbled as he handed them over and picked up his lunch box.

B.J. hadn't carried one since the day she'd found the dead lizard, preferring to manage with whatever food could be kept in her backpack without spoilage rather than giving Dana Thomas a chance to repeat his nasty surprise.

The air in the villa had been frigid the past four evenings in spite of the tropical heat as Dana and B.J., without verbal discussion, had worked out a system of avoidance. He ate dinner while she showered. She moved to the kitchen, and he claimed the bath. He watched the evening news while she did her personal laundry, hanging it in her room. She remained there, studying prints spread on her bed, sometimes tempted to ask him to explain something that was unclear but stubbornly resisting the impulse.

One evening, he had gone to the pool and images of the night she had lost herself in his arms filled her head. She could still feel his mouth on hers and his body pressed against her. Only fate had prevented them from making a terrible mistake, but to resort to putting a dead lizard in her lunch because she had refused to continue their folly after she'd come to her senses had been pathetic.

She turned the ignition over then gunned the car out of the parking space and down the steep hill with a vengeance. She sensibly slowed when she reached the highway. She heard the man beside her give a barely audible sigh of relief and saw his feet, which had been planted firmly on the floorboard, visibly relax.

"Glad you got that, whatever it was, out of your system, Sutherland," he growled.

"The only systems you need to concern yourself with at the moment are at ChemCorp, Thomas," she retorted.

"I'll concern myself with the performance of *any* system that threatens my safety, Sutherland."

"Oh, you're perfectly safe with me, Thomas," she said

with exaggerated emphasis.

Her double-entendre was not lost on Dana, and he was left with no suitable repartee that would not get him into deeper waters, so he remained silent for the remainder of the drive.

From the corner of his eye, Dana watched the obstinate woman behind the wheel. The early morning sun cast a golden glow on her fine-featured face, and he felt a sudden urge to reach out and stroke the back of her arched neck—after he wrung it, of course for doubting his denial of pulling that cruel prank on her. That she thought him capable of doing a thing like that was insulting enough but refusing to accept his word that he had not was the last straw. The past few days had been full of tension, and he was looking forward to the time when their evenings playing house together were over. Monday couldn't come too soon.

At the end of the day, Albert Zurow called the operators together in his office. He glanced at B.J., standing just inside the door and opened his mouth, then thought better of it, and seated himself in the crowded room's only chair.

"Well, men—ah, people—after the weekend you'll begin carrying shifts. I've been quite pleased with your break-in performance." Here he looked directly at B.J. as though it was necessary to acknowledge that his negative expectations had been in error. "I feel confident that you are ready to put the systems in operation. Anyone disagree?"

"We're ready," Pete Marshall assured him. "Right, guys?"

"And gal," Frank Kelly reminded him. "Don't forget our petticoat section."

"If you are referring to me, Kelly," B.J. said evenly, "I'm wearing jeans the same as you. But I *am* ready."

"I'll just bet you are, Miss Sutherland." Frank answered and the other men laughed while B.J. felt her cheeks flame.

His meaning had been very clear, and Dana wanted to punch his leering face but reminded himself that B.J. didn't deserve his protection. She thought she needed protecting from him.

Albert Zurow cleared his throat and shuffled the papers on his desk before he spoke again. "Obviously, one man, uh person, in each villa will be on days while the other works nights. Anyone have a preference for Monday's shift? Miss Sutherland?"

"No preference," she said flatly.

"I'll take nights," Dana offered.

"Same for me," Pete Marshall said.

"Me, too," Yancy Webb added.

"Okay, we'll start off with Sutherland and Kelly carrying day shift Monday, Thomas and Marshall night, and Webb and Evans off. And since the people relieving shifts will need transportation, I'll expect each group to work out who rides with whom," Zurow continued. "So that's all. Have a good weekend."

As the group reached the hallway, Frank Kelly caught up with B.J. "How about if I pick you up Monday morning?"

"Thanks, but I thought I'd drive."

"Okay by me, sweets, so you pick me up. I'm easy."

B.J. knew she was boxed into a corner. Either way, she was stuck with Frank Kelly, not only during her shift but also to and from the job. "Fine." She hitched her backpack onto her shoulders and turned toward the door leading outside.

"Come by early, just in case we run out of gas, sweets," Frank grinned and punched Marshall in the arm with his elbow.

B.J. stopped, turned slowly to face the group of men behind her, and fixed Kelly with a level gaze. "I'm B.J. or Sutherland, but I'm *not* sweets. Also, the only gas we might run out of is the kind coming out of your mouth, Kelly, and I would welcome that." Amid the laughter of the men, she wheeled around and bolted out the door.

Dana would have applauded her performance in cutting Frank Kelly down to size if he hadn't been still smarting from the scissors job she'd done on him that morning.

B.J. was glad she didn't have to make small talk on the drive back to the villa. While Dana fought the heavy afternoon traffic, she battled with her tumultuous emotions. She shouldn't have let Frank Kelly get to her, but the man had badgered her since day one. She knew his type well enough and had managed to fend them off during the training program and her first job but letting her guard down with Dana Thomas had left her vulnerable. She'd sworn never to let that happen again. Proving herself a competent operator would take all her effort and concentration. She couldn't afford to be diverted from her goal.

B.J. glanced sideways at the man sitting behind the

wheel, reminding herself that she couldn't let herself get dis-
tracted by an attractive man like her house-mate. She was
well aware that he could make her forget everything when
she was in his arms.

The phone was ringing when she unlocked the door to
the villa. Dana, carrying both lunch box and brief case was
trailing behind her, so B.J. took the call. When she said hello
a young female voice answered. "Oh, sorry, I must have the
wrong number. I was calling Dana Thomas."

"You have his number," she answered as she turned toward the man who stood waiting in the middle of the room.
"He's right here." She held the receiver toward him, smiling
sweetly. "It's for you."

B.J. went to the refrigerator and took out a pitcher of iced
tea and poured a glassful. Then she busied herself making a
tuna sandwich. There was no way she was going to miss this
conversation. It would be interesting to see how Dana Thomas
talked his way out of this situation. For a moment she almost
felt sorry for him, trapped as he was, but then she remembered how he had embraced her in the pool and her sympathy
evaporated faster than the ice cubes in her frosted glass.

Dana listened for a long moment, then said, "Is this
really necessary right now? Can't we work something out to
avoid it for the time being?" He spoke in terse sentences that
gave away nothing of the subject under discussion.

She supposed he was a pro at this, having probably been
caught before. More than likely the woman on the other end
of the line was used to forgiving him and letting him have
one more chance. Well, at least she had not been that kind
of fool. Not that Tom has asked her to take him back, she
suddenly remembered. Maybe that was what had hurt the
most. He'd simply asked for a divorce and walked away,
leaving her to put her life back together. B.J. was so lost in
her own memories that she failed to realize Dana had terminated his conversation until he spoke close behind her.

"I'll be flying out of here in the morning, if I can arrange
it. Would you mind taking me to the airport?"

"Of course. I mean, no, I wouldn't mind." B.J. felt the
color rising in her flustered face as she turned to look at him,
aware that she had violated his privacy by listening.

"I'll be gone all week," he went on. "So Webb will have to
fill in for me." He suddenly looked drawn and tired.

She had an impulsive desire to smooth the lines from his face. Instead, she filled a second glass with tea and held it out to him.

He took it with an absent-minded nod of thanks and continued talking, almost as if to himself. "I suppose I'd better call Zurow first. He's not going to be happy to be short an operator right now."

B.J. couldn't resist one last barb. "Couldn't you talk yourself out of this one, Thomas?"

"Not unless I want to face a contempt of court charge." He turned and walked toward his bedroom without waiting for her reaction.

Court? Why was he required to be in court? Divorce proceedings? A custody hearing? Child support? Whatever it was had happened before she'd answered the phone. Whatever it was about, the man surely deserved the summons. She was thankful she'd had the good sense to stay out of his life. With a shudder, she thought of how close she'd come to trusting Dana Thomas with her heart, but she hadn't and that was the bottom line.

Arriving at Alexander Hamilton Airport for the second time that day, B.J. was already regretting her impulsive invitation of the night before. After learning that Dana Thomas would be away for several days, she had decided this would be an opportune time to have her parents join her for a visit.

George and Matilda Lindsey lived in Atlanta and had already stated their wishes to come to St. Croix while she was here. Having a male house-mate had created a sticky situation, and she hadn't been sure just how she was going to get around that until presented with Dana's current trip to the States.

Since the Lindseys were retired, the impromptu invitation had been accepted, and they were arriving on the afternoon flight to the island. Fortunately, her house-mate had taken most of his personal belongings with him, and what he'd left she had tucked out of sight in her own closet.

In honor of the occasion, she was wearing one of the few

skirts she had brought, a softly flared denim, and a white knit top. Her deeply tanned neck and arms were bare of jewelry, and her only makeup was a touch of lip gloss. A low drone caught her attention, and she moved to the large terminal windows that overlooked the airfield just in time to see the plane come to a bumpy stop on the short runway. B.J. wiped her hands on her skirt and went forward to meet the arriving passengers, dreading the inspection and interrogation she was sure would follow.

"Betty Jo, darling! Over here." Her mother was waving frantically as B.J. walked toward customs.

B.J. returned the greeting as she waited for her parents to be checked through.

"How's my girl?" her father asked as he put down the two large bags he carried and hugged her hard.

"Great, Dad," she said, her words muffled against his broad chest as she returned his embrace.

Then she bent to kiss her petite mother's cool cheek. "You look fabulous, as always, Mother." She reached for her mother's carry-on. "Just follow me. The car is right outside."

"How brown you've gotten, Betty Jo." Matilda shook her head. "You'll have a million wrinkles before you're my age."

B.J. laughed. "I work in the sun, Mother. And ChemCorp wouldn't approve my wearing a sunbonnet instead of a hard hat."

"You look like a golfer, honey," George commented with a wink as he hoisted the heavy bags again.

"You ought to know, Dad. How's your game these days?"

"Not too bad. I broke eighty yesterday. How's yours?"

"I've only had one chance to play since I got here, but I won a few bucks off the guy I played with. We'll have to play—"

"A man? Oh, how nice. Will we get to meet him, Betty Jo?"

"Afraid not, Mother. And don't get your hopes up. It was just a guy I work with." She thought of Dana Thomas' dark good looks and wished for a moment she could introduce him to her parents as the new man in her life. Then she remembered the real reason she couldn't. "Besides, he's married." B.J. lifted the hatchback and helped her dad arrange the luggage.

"We really are only staying a few days, honey, but you

know your mother travels with a complete wardrobe for every contingency."

"I'm afraid I'll only have the weekend to take you around the island, then it's back to work."

"Don't worry, darling. I'm sure your dad and I will find plenty to do and see while you are at that job, though why on earth you ever wanted to become a power plant worker when you could have had a nice job at the bank like your sister is beyond my wildest imagination. It's so—so—"

"Unladylike?" B.J. supplied as they played the scene from a script that she now knew by heart. She climbed into the driver's seat as her father helped her mother into the back.

Her father sat beside B.J. in the front. "I think it's a hoot. My daughter, B.J. the operator. I'll bet that showed Tom Sutherland a thing or two."

"Our daughter's name is Betty Jo," Matilda said firmly. "It's not enough she's doing a man's job, now she's using a man's name. What on earth are people going to think?"

"That I'm just one of the guys, Mother," B.J. said wryly thinking of all her mother's wasted efforts in teaching her to be a perfect wife. Well, she'd been that, but Tom had left her anyway. She had even let him beat her at golf, but that hadn't kept him happy either. "By the way, how is my big sis?"

"She's still waiting for the divorce to become final."

Matilda sighed audibly. "She sends you her love."

Racine had just split with her second husband and was going through a very acrimonious divorce settlement quite unlike the quick and quiet end of her own marriage to Tom.

Heading the Escort toward Christiansted she thought of the trip earlier today and wondered if Dana Thomas had reached his destination. She wondered just what he faced when he got there. He had not chosen to explain his reasons for going, but she was certain it had to do with marital problems and thought again how glad she was that his problems had nothing to do with her.

When they reached the villa, Matilda gasped at the sight of the locked gate and barred windows. "Oh, my, I didn't expect this. Are you sure it's safe here?"

"Quite safe, Mother. These villas are vacant much of the time, and it's just a precaution against vandalism."

"Atlanta is hot in the summertime, but St. Croix is hotter," George observed as they climbed out of the car.

"The trade wind tempers the heat here. We don't even use air conditioners." B.J. unlocked the door and ushered her parents inside.

Matilda gave the room a quick, appraising glance. "It is quite tasteful, isn't it? I like the tropical look."

"Where do these go?" George asked, still holding the bags and perspiring heavily.

"Oh, sorry, Dad." B.J. led the way to Dana's bedroom. "In here." Her eyes swept the room nervously, searching for any telltale evidence of her house-mate that she might have overlooked earlier. Seeing none, she relaxed and went to close the shutters against the afternoon sun.

"I don't think you've mentioned who is sharing your villa, Betty Jo. Had you met her before?" Matilda asked as she sat down on the bed and removed her sunglasses and wide-brimmed hat.

"No, I didn't know Dana Thomas until I came here." B.J. told the truth, just not all of it.

"Thomas?" Matilda smiled. "There's a Thomas family in banking in Atlanta. Could she be related? Where is she from?"

B.J. smiled at her mother's habit of asking two questions at once. "I don't think so, and I don't know, in that order."

"You've been sharing a place with this woman for two weeks, and you don't know where she's from?" Matilda looked aghast.

That's not the half of it, B.J. thought wryly. She knew her mother took family background very seriously, and she sought to make amends for her faux pas. "We've been busy with our break-in, Mother. There hasn't been time for small talk."

"Speaking of time," George cut in, "Shouldn't we be thinking about lunch? I'm starved."

"Right," B.J. said, relieved to change the subject, "I thought we'd drive over to the Buccaneer and have their buf-fet. After we eat, I can show you the golf course I played, Dad. Maybe we can get in a game tomorrow while Mother checks out all the Christiansted shops."

"Sounds good to me." George picked up his billed golfing cap and looked at his wife. "Ready?"

"I should change into something else," Matilda told him.

"Now, sweetheart." He put an arm around her tiny waist,

"You look wonderful. There'll be plenty of time later to wear all those pretty clothes you brought."

B.J. headed back to the car before her mother could protest. She was beginning to wonder if this had been such a good idea. Two grueling weeks of break-in had left her in no state to fend her mother's probing questions, and she must keep her house-mate's true identity from being discovered at all costs.

The parking lot at the Buccaneer was not crowded, and B.J. easily found a space. As she led the way toward The Terrace, she was reminded how she had lingered here all last Saturday afternoon with Dana, basking in his open admiration of her. B.J. slammed the car door with more force than necessary as she made an effort to also close her mind to his appealing image. Why, oh why couldn't the man stay out of her head?

"It's lovely," Matilda pronounced as she glanced toward the Caribbean.

"Great golf course," George added. "I'm looking forward—"

"Well, if it isn't Miss Sutherland."

B.J. whirled around at the sound of the familiar voice and found herself facing Frank Kelly and Pete Marshall. Oh, no. She hadn't remembered that they might be here again today.

"Hi, guys," she said with a nervous smile and kept walking toward The Terrace.

"Hey, did Thomas get away this morning?" Pete asked.

"Sure did," she answered and almost pushed her parents toward the restaurant entrance.

"Do you know what that emergency business was all about?" Pete called after her.

"Don't have a clue." She shrugged apologetically and turned toward the maître d. "Table for three, please."

"Probably monkey business." Frank slapped Pete on the back and both men laughed as they walked away.

"Well, who was that?" Matilda asked curiously as soon as

they were seated.

"Just a couple of guys I work with," B.J. said. "I didn't think it worth the time to introduce you."

"Was one the man you played golf with?" Matilda persisted.

"No, it wasn't." She motioned to the waiter who was passing by their table. "I can recommend the buffet, but we need to decide on drinks." Her voice sounded almost normal for a person whose heart had leaped into her throat. That had been a close call. She could just imagine the story those guys would have told if they'd witnessed her mother's shocked reaction to learning that her daughter was living with a man she worked with. She would have to make sure nothing like this happened again.

Vaguely she wondered how her husband had managed to live a life of deception for months or maybe years. He must have had more guts that she gave him credit for. That thought brought her to Dana Thomas. Did he get some perverse pleasure in living on the edge of discovery, too? Well, Mister Thomas seemed about to pay the price for whatever indiscretions he'd engaged in, and she figured it was well deserved. With a sigh, she willed her thoughts back to the present and her role as hostess to her visiting parents.

CHAPTER SIX

Coming out of Tampa International Airport, Dana hailed a cab and gave the address in Gulf Vista Estates. He had kept the house, newly purchased just before the accident, and each return had been a painful reminder of all that he had lost. It would have been wise to sell it, he knew, but each time he convinced himself to do it, the thought of destroying the last remnants of his family life stopped him.

Now he was facing the trauma of a court case that had been pending ever since the plane crashed two years ago. It was a score he was anxious to settle and had almost given up hope of happening. He should have explained this to B.J. before he left, but her reaction to his attorney's call had put him off. It was obvious she had jumped to another wrong conclusion about him, and he wasn't sure she would have believed the truth if he'd told her. Somebody must have betrayed her big time to leave her suspicious of every male alive. If it was that guy from IPPS why would she choose to work for the same company herself? Maybe he would just have to ask her that when he got back.

The cab pulled into the familiar driveway. Dana paid the driver and got out. His feet felt like lead as he walked to the front door, unlocked it, and went inside. The foyer was as dim and quiet as a tomb. He crossed the living room to the wide glass doors and jerked open the vertical blind, revealing a view of the patio and the gym set beyond. Dana closed his eyes as a painfully sharp image of Kate pushing Jared on the swing flashed across his mind. He unfastened the latch and went outside, walking slowly to the slide where his son had played. For a long moment he stood, running his hand over the brightly painted metal, now rusting slightly from the humidity. He sighed regretfully, then went inside to make a call.

Victoria Harper had cancelled a luncheon date after receiving Dana Thomas' call. Within half an hour, she announced her presence at the gates of Gulf Vista Estates. She had planned to meet with him on Sunday to discuss his court appearance the following day, but he had asked her to come today.

Dana met her at the front door with a friendly hug. "Hi, Vickie. How've you been?"

"Great, Dan. And you?"

"Okay." Dana winced. Nobody but Kate and Victoria had ever called him that. He led her to the snack bar that separated the family room from the kitchen. "Something to drink?"

"Sure, whatever you have."

"There's Sprite and beer."

"Sprite's fine."

Dana placed a can and glass of ice cubes on the counter then popped the top on a beer for himself.

"I've made a decision, Vickie, and I want to put it in motion before I change my mind."

"Okay?" She looked at him expectantly.

"I'm going to sell the house. I'd like you to take care of it. Furniture, too. If there's anything here you'd like, for yourself or Ian, please take it."

"Well, thanks. I'd be pleased to have something of Kate's in my house, and I'm sure Ian would like a keepsake of Jared's."

"How is the little guy?" Ian had been his son's best friend just as Victoria was Kate's. The boys had spent a lot of time together after they'd bought the house.

"Growing like Kudzu and about as wild." Victoria shook her head. "I'm counting on kindergarten to settle him down."

Dana winced again. Jared would have been starting

school, too. It was why Kate had wanted the house.

"That hurt. I'm sorry," Victoria said softly.

"It's okay," Dana told her. "I just keep wishing I hadn't insisted that they come on the job to Saudi, but we had agreed that in a couple of years Kate would stay home with Jared. I wanted them with me this one last job."

"Stop punishing yourself, Dan. It wasn't your fault crazy terrorists blew up the plane. You shouldn't be punishing yourself. You should be feeling relieved. They're finally going to pay for it."

"It won't change what they did," Dana said flatly, "but if there's any monetary settlement, I've been thinking of what I want to do with it. I'd like to establish a Jared Thomas Fund for homeless children."

"How wonderful, Dan," Victoria said sincerely.

"Kate would have wanted that."

"Dan," Victoria reached across the counter and touched his arm. "I may be out of line here, but I think it's time to get on with your life. Go out with someone, maybe marry again. You've got to bring closure to what happened."

"Right. Maybe when the court case is over I can do that."

"I think Kate would want you to be happy. Life is for the living, cruel as it may seem. She wouldn't want to see you like this."

Dana nodded solemnly. "Vickie, can I ask you something?"

Victoria smiled at him. "As my client or my friend?"

"Both, maybe. I need to know how you feel about men, in general, after what Nathan did to you."

"Well..." Victoria knit her brows while she considered the question. "At first, I think I hated all of them, but I got over it. Of course, meeting another man I could care for helped."

"Then you think if a woman meets the right guy she can love someone else?"

"I would say yes." She took a sip of her Sprite and studied him over the top of her glass. "Hey, this is beginning to sound like more than just a general question. May I ask something now? Have you met someone, Dan?"

"Yeah, you could say that." He thought of B.J. with her obstinate refusal to let him get beyond the barrier she had erected around herself. "But I don't know what to do about it."

"Unless the woman is crazy, you'll only have to whistle."

Dana shook his head in denial. "It will take a lot more than whistling to impress this one."

"I think you're underestimating yourself, friend. You'd be a prize catch for any woman. So if you're interested in her, let her know. I'm sure it will work out."

Dana grinned. "Are you making this statement as my attorney or my friend?"

"Both." Victoria stood and slung her stylish leather bag over her shoulder. "I've got to run now. I need to see the real estate agency about listing the house, so it can make tomorrow's paper." She looked at Dana for a long moment. "Are you sure this is what you want to do, Dan?"

"I'm sure," he answered firmly.

After he saw Victoria to her car, Dana stood watching her drive away.

Vickie had been the victim of a lousy husband, but she was still all woman. She had never tried to deny it or be one of the guys.

He thought of B.J. with her jeans and boyish haircut and determination to do a man's job. Maybe all she needed was someone to prove to her that she was still a woman in spite of all her efforts to deny it, and a desirable woman at that. He had tried already, but maybe he needed to try harder. She was the woman he wanted, and he'd have to convince her of it.

"Okay, Miss Sutherland, you can fire the burners now," Frank Kelly said loudly as he and the two operator trainees came into the control room.

B.J. looked up from the control board. "You found the problem?"

"It was just a careless mistake." Frank took the chair next to B.J. and swiveled to look at her. "You left a switch open on a row of igniters."

"No, I didn't," B.J. told him with certainty. "They were all closed when I took my lunch break." She looked at the nearest trainee. "That's why I gave Lohr the go ahead to fire while I was gone."

"I'm sure you *thought* so, but like I told the men..." He looked from one to the other. "It pays to double-check things. We wasted time tracing that open switch today."

"It was closed, Kelly. I double-checked," B.J. insisted. "This is not my first rodeo."

"I never thought it was, Miss Sutherland," Frank said in a placating tone. "I'm sure you've had lots of experience."

B.J. pressed her lips tightly together to keep back the reply that clamored to burst out. She would not stoop to the level of bickering with Frank Kelly in front of the trainees, no matter how much he baited her. But just because she was a woman, did he have to give a sexual innuendo to everything that came up? The control room was stifling, in spite of being air-conditioned. She pushed back her chair. "Desmond, take over here. I need a break."

"Yes, miss." The man slid into her vacated place.

"Take your time in the powder room, Miss Sutherland," Frank called after her. "We'll try and manage without your experienced help."

Without answering, B.J. slammed the door and leaned against it. The man was impossible, and she didn't know how much more of his badgering she could take without exploding. When Dana, got back she would ask him to change shifts with her.

"Everything all right, Miss Sutherland?"

B.J. opened her eyes to see Albert Zurow looking at her with concern.

"Fine." She forced a smile. "I just needed a break."

"Frank Kelly told me about the problem with the igniters. Try to be more careful, Miss Sutherland."

"But I—" She stopped, realizing she was talking to Zurow's back as he went into the control room and the door closed behind him. "So much for a fair hearing," she mumbled under her breath as she headed down the hall, counting the hours till the work day was over.

B.J. unlocked the gate to the villa and let herself in, recognizing the aroma of her mother's spaghetti sauce before she reached the kitchen.

"Mmmmm, smells good, Mother." She put down her backpack and kissed her mother's moist cheek. "But you didn't need to cook dinner. I was planning to take you out someplace fancy for your last night here."

"I thought you needed a home-cooked meal, dear. I know you aren't eating right, working such long hours."

"Where's Dad?" B.J. asked as she washed her hands and prepared to chop the vegetables her mother had already as-sembled for the salad.

"Still at the pool." Matilda sighed. "I keep reminding him the sun is hotter here than in Atlanta, but he just goes on baking himself." After a moment of silence, she asked, "How was work today? Are you as exhausted as you look?"

Awful and yes, B.J. was tempted to blurt out, but instead made an effort to lighten up. "It was okay and probably not."

Matilda picked up a stalk of celery and began to chop in neat even strokes. "Betty Jo, there's something I'd like to talk with you about."

The tone of her mother's voice alerted B.J. that this was no ordinary chat, and she prepared herself for the inevitable.

"Today when I was looking in your closet for a longer cover-up for the pool, I saw...a man's things. Your dad said I should just keep out of it, but I'm your mother, and I know how vulnerable a woman in...your position can be." Matilda finished the celery and picked up a carrot. "Betty Jo, are you having an affair with that married man you play golf with?"

B.J. laughed, relieved at not being found out after all. "No, Mother. Absolutely not. I just—well, a guy I work with left some things here when he went home on emergency leave."

It was all true, just not all of the truth, but her mother looked skeptical. "I'll be giving them back as soon as he re-turns."

Matilda closed her eyes dramatically. "Only two daugh-ters and both divorced. And your sister has already made the same mistake twice. I just hope you don't follow her exam-ple, Betty Jo."

"Not to worry, Mother, since I have no plans to marry again...ever." This time she spoke with the conviction of tell-ing the whole truth.

"I can't see why both of you couldn't find a man like your father. All of them have been nice Atlanta boys from good families. I just don't understand it."

"Maybe that's our problem," B.J. said with mock serious-ness. "Maybe Dad was the last good man in Atlanta."

"This is no laughing matter, darling. I do worry what kind of men you are associating with now on that job. I'm sure they must be crude and—"

"Not all of them, Mother, just a few." B.J. thought of Frank Kelly. "You taught me how to be a lady, even in jeans and a hard hat." She patted her mother's hand to reassure her. "Now why don't I take a quick shower while you go out to the pool and bring Dad back? It would be a shame to keep such a nice dinner waiting."

Appeased, Matilda did as suggested while B.J. shed her dusty jeans and headed for the bathroom. *Another close call.* After trying unsuccessfully to defend her competency at work, she hadn't felt up to defending her virtue at home. She would have been even less likely to convince her mother she was not at fault than any of the men she worked with.

CHAPTER SEVEN

B.J. had worn her denim skirt again to the airport but carefully avoided examining her motive. What did she care if Dana Thomas thought of her as one of the guys? That was what she wanted him to think. He hadn't asked her to meet his plane today, but since she was off it seemed the right thing to do.

The late afternoon humidity had left her short hair in soft tendrils about her face, which she had made up with more care than usual. She had substituted a brighter lipstick for her transparent gloss and added a touch of eye shadow the blue-green color of her eyes.

Looking impatiently at her watch, B.J. realized the plane was late. A worried frown crossed her face, then she gave herself a mental shake. It was silly to worry. The man could certainly take care of himself.

It had been two days since her parents left.

She had put Dana's room back in order the way it had been before their visit. Moving his things, she had been overwhelmed by the feelings they evoked in her. Her housemate's presence was overpowering even when he was miles away, and when she thought of why he was away it had brought her back to the real world faster than the speed of light. She'd been there, done that, and had the divorce papers to prove it.

"What am I doing here?" she asked herself softly. "Maybe I should just go back to the villa and let Dana Thomas get a cab when he arrives."

Before she could convince herself that was the wise thing to do, the intercom squawked out the arrival of Flight 403 from Miami, and it was too late. She hurried toward Customs to make sure Dana saw her before he looked for a cab, and at the sight of him, her heart rate went into double-time.

His face appeared haggard, and his jawline was dark with a day's growth of beard. None of that kept him from being the most attractive man she had ever known.

"Dana, over here," she said as he lifted his duffle bag from the conveyer and turned the opposite way. He reversed direction and at the sight of her, a smile to die for lit his handsome features.

"B.J." He reached out and gave her a comradely hug with his free arm. "I wasn't expecting you."

She shrugged with exaggerated nonchalance, while the warmth where his arm had touched her bare skin washed over her entire body. "I had the day off and the car, so I thought you could use a lift."

"It's a lift in more ways than one to find you waiting," he said softly, his eyes holding hers in a lingering caress.

"Come on," she said breathlessly as she broke the mesmerizing contact. "The car's this way."

B.J. got into the driver's seat as Dana slid in beside her, tossing his battered bag into the back. With a trembling hand, she reached for the ignition, then gripped the gear shift more tightly than necessary to cover the visible effect he had on her. She wanted to ask him how his trip had been, but from the looks of him that would be a mistake. When in doubt, don't, she reminded herself and kept silent. But it was a silence as heavy with tension as with the afternoon heat. She was aware of this man in every fiber of her being, and despite knowing that he was trouble with a capital "T" she wanted him. What he was didn't seem to matter to her body, and her mind was powerless in the face of her need. Only love could make a woman feel that way, but she was afraid to admit that she loved this man.

Finally Dana broke the silence. "How are things going at the plant?"

"Okay." She took a deep breath, glad to be back on safe ground for the present.

"All the equipment functioning well?"

"Off and on. No major problems so far. The trainees are

trying to learn, but they'll need watching for a while yet. Desmond or Lohr, I'm not sure which, left a switch open on a row of igniters Friday, and we lost a lot of time."

"Did Zurow go ballistic?"

"He might have, if he'd thought it was one of his own, but he got the impression I did it." Her voice betrayed the resentment she still felt at the injustice of it.

"Oh? What made him think that?"

"I'm not sure." Better not to make accusations when she wasn't certain. It could have been either of the three men, and the other two would have covered even if they'd known.

"What do you say we stop for something to eat?" Dana offered. "I haven't had any decent food all day." He raised a hand to his unshaven jaw. "Unless you'd rather not be seen with me in a public place right now?"

"You look okay," she said, and added silently, much more than okay to me. "Anything special you had in mind?"

Dana thought for a moment. "I'd like a nice, thick steak, and I know a good place to get it. Have you ever been to the Cormorant Beach Club?"

When B.J. shook her head, Dana continued, "Turn left onto Granard Road and that'll take you to Route 75, then hang a right at the Texaco Station and head toward the beach."

"Got it," B.J. said and concentrated on watching the road signs. She was glad for a delay in facing the intimacy of the villa. Perhaps by the time they'd had dinner and talked, she could overcome her desire to give him the kind of welcome home she was fantasizing right now.

The Cormorant Beach Club was almost deserted this early on Monday evening, and they were given their choice of seating. Dana motioned toward a table next to the water and asked, "Is that one okay?"

"Lovely," she answered and followed the waiter toward it.

The sun was just setting, and Dana used that reason to take the chair adjacent to B.J. rather than opposite. "We'll have a great view of the sunset from here."

His arm was almost touching hers, and B.J. shivered from the nearness. She had never felt this intense longing for contact with another person, not even Tom in the days of their brief courtship. It did no good to tell herself that Dana Thomas was a married man. But maybe he wasn't, after his trip to the States, she thought hopefully.

They placed their orders. Dana chose steak, B.J. fish. Then they sat sipping their mimosas while they waited for dinner to be served. The Caribbean waters had become a deep purple now, and sailboats returning to Christiansted harbor were dark silhouettes against the crimson sky. The gentle lapping of the waves, synchronized with the trade wind, had a hypnotic effect, which was enhanced by the fragrant scent of tropical flowers that surrounded the terrace overlooking the sea.

B.J. suddenly wished that she could hold this moment in time forever. It felt so right to be here with this man. He had come back, and nothing else seemed to matter.

"It's good to be back," Dana said sincerely.

B.J. met his eyes, read his unspoken words, *I've missed you*, then looked away.

"I hope you didn't get too accustomed to having a private villa," he said softly.

"Actually, I wasn't alone most of the time. I thought while you were away was a convenient time to ask my parents to come for a visit, so I did."

When Dana didn't respond, B.J. went on. "They used your room, but I've put everything back in order. I suppose I should have asked you first, but it was a spur of the moment invitation. I hope you don't mind?"

"No, I don't mind," he assured her. "Where are they from?"

"Atlanta. Dad's a retired investment counselor. Now he's a full time golfer."

Dana grinned. "That explains a lot of things. And your mom?"

"Oh, my mother wouldn't be caught dead on a golf course. Too much sun."

"Daddy's girl. I should have figured. Are you their only child?" Dana asked.

"No, I have an older sister. Racine is my mother's daughter, a real Southern Belle."

Dana was about to ask another question but their dinner arrived just then, and they gave their attention to the food.

A band tuned up at the far end of the terrace and began to play old familiar songs. Perhaps it was the bottle of wine they shared with their meal that added the final impetus to make B.J. bolder than she had ever been. She wanted to dance with Dana, wanted to be held in his arms, and she decided not to wait for him to do the asking.

"I want to dance with you." She held out her hand in a tentative invitation.

"Then you shall." Dana pushed back his chair and led her to the tiny dance floor adjacent to the band.

B.J. moved into his arms as if she'd done it a thousand times instead of only once before. It felt right to be there, so right. *I won't think of love*, she told herself. *I know he doesn't love me. I will only think of satisfying this terrible longing to be close to him. That will be enough.*

The band was playing "Just The Way You Are", and she thought how it no longer mattered to her what he had been before this place in time. She closed her eyes and laid her cheek against Dana's stubble-covered jaw.

Dana pulled her closer, so that their bodies were touching from shoulder to knee. *She fit perfectly*, he thought, as if she was made for his arms. Her face was almost on a level with his own, so that when she raised her eyes to look at him, she didn't have to tilt her head as Kate had done. She was his equal, in every way. And tonight he needed her in all the ways a man could need a woman.

The band segued into "When A Man Loves A Woman", and he realized that in spite of all he'd been through this past week or maybe because of it, he had reached a milestone. He knew what he wanted now. He wanted this woman, and he sensed that she felt the same way. He didn't know what had caused the change in her since he had returned, but he wasn't about to question it.

The song was still playing when he asked huskily in her ear, "Ready?"

"Yes." Her whispered answer told him that she understood the real meaning of his question.

He drove them to the villa, one hand on the wheel, the other holding hers. Neither spoke, as if afraid of breaking the spell that enveloped them in the silence.

He parked the car, and she slid out the driver's side, not letting go of his hand. At the gate, he fumbled with the key, still holding to her as he unlocked the door. Neither reached for the light switch as they entered the house, only hesitating for a moment in the hallway between their bedrooms. Then he turned her toward him and cupped her face in his hands. Slowly he kissed her eyelids, then each cheek.

He wanted her—all of her—with a fierceness he had never felt before. He wanted her, not just for tonight, but for all the nights to come. He would make sure she understood what he was feeling before he made love to her in every way he knew how. His lips found hers, and he pressed her closer, feeling her shiver of anticipation as she wrapped her arms around his neck. "I want you," he whispered huskily.

His words seemed to have a sobering effect on her emotions. She pushed back from his embrace and said softly, "Just for the record, I want you to know I don't expect anything from you. I don't know what you've done in the past or who you've been involved with, but it doesn't matter. All that matters to me is now. Whatever happens between us here will be enough. When this job is over, we'll go our separate ways, and that will be the end of it. No strings attached."

Her words were like a splash of ice water, chilling his ardor completely, then replacing it with hot anger. "So that's the way you see me, see what we have between us. Well, as long as we're setting the record straight here, I should tell you that I'm not looking for a one night stand. Nor a one job stand either."

"Isn't that supposed to be my line, Thomas?"

"Not necessarily, since you seem to prefer being just one of the guys, Sutherland."

" I thought you went back to the States because of marital problems of some sort and—"

"And you're willing to overlook my past and play house while we're sharing this villa together?"

"Yes, I am. You said you wanted me, and I want you. I thought we could have what we wanted with no strings attached."

"You think too much. And you jump to a lot of wrong conclusions. You never give me the benefit of the doubt, do you? You've got me pegged as a womanizer like that guy in your past, and you won't let go of it. So thanks but no thanks. I'm looking for a woman I can share my life with. I was hoping it could have been you, but I can see I was mistaken." He turned and went into his bedroom, closing the door behind him.

B.J. stood in the dark hallway, hands over her mouth to

stop the agonized protests that struggled to get out. She had thought she was offering what he wanted. How could she have known he was looking for a permanent relationship? How could she know that for sure now? Maybe he always told a woman that. *Here I go again*, she said silently. Mistrusting his motives. But love was a gamble, a calculated risk, and she had been hurt badly before. Would the result this time have been worth taking the chance he expected her to take? Now she would never know.

After he showered, Dana lay awake in the dark, too tired to sleep. The week had been a nightmare as he was forced to relive the senseless act of violence that had claimed the lives of his wife and child. Then he had sorted through the contents of the house, which had evoked more painful memories as he kept asking himself why he'd insisted that Kate join him in Saudi. If only he hadn't, both Kate and Jared would be alive now. And finally, he had come to terms with the fact that he couldn't undo the past, that they were gone from him forever. He'd finally accepted that he had a life ahead of him and it was not a betrayal of what he'd shared with Kate to love again.

Then his thoughts had turned to Betty Jo Sutherland, and he had realized for the first time that what he felt for her was more than just a physical attraction; it was love. A love he hoped that she returned, and for a while tonight he felt it to be true. Then she'd laid out the rules for their relationship, just like she'd set the rules for their living arrangements in the villa. Her lack of trust in him had come through loud and clear. He couldn't build a life with a woman who had no faith in him, who refused to believe the best of him unless proven otherwise. Her offer to overlook his supposed offenses had been too much. With those grim thoughts in mind , the hum of the overhead fan finally lulled him into oblivion.

In her room across the hall, B.J. tossed and turned, trying to sort out in her mind what she had learned. Dana hadn't said he loved her, but he had said he was looking for a woman to spend the rest of his life with. If only she hadn't told him she was willing to settle for so much less. She had thought commitment was out of the question, and her feelings for him had driven her to compromise her scruples in order to have something rather than nothing. She had dared once again to open her heart to someone. And once again she was left with nothing.

Outside, a night bird called to its mate, and she shivered at the lonely sound of it. Then she heard it again and realized that it was coming from Dana's room. Something was wrong. Not taking time to put on her robe, she ran across the hall in her long t-shirt and stopped at the closed door.

The sound came again, an agonized muffled sob, and without hesitation, she opened the door and went to the bed where he lay.

"Kate! Kate," he yelled as he thrashed about, waving his arms. "Don't go!" He covered his head with his pillow. "No, oh no."

"Dana," she put her hands on his shoulders and shook him gently. "Wake up. You're having a nightmare."

"Huh?" He tried to sit up, but she sat on the side of the bed and held him against her.

"Shhh. It's all right." She felt the heat of his body and his wildly beating heart and knew he had come back to reality from something terrifying.

"Kate?"

"I'm not Kate," she said softly. "My name is Betty Jo." She wasn't even aware of using her real name.

"No." He shook his head, "Kate is dead."

"Dead?" she held her breath, willing him to say more.

"In the crash." He reached for the lamp beside his bed and switched it on. The light seemed to bring him wide awake. "I must have been dreaming," he said and brushed at the lock of hair that clung to his damp forehead.

"You were talking in your sleep," she told him as she moved away from him but remained seated on the bed. "Actually, you were yelling. I came to see what was wrong."

He shifted the pillows behind him and sat up, being careful to keep his body covered with the sheet.

She realized that he must have nothing on but she was focused on something else at the moment. "Who's Kate?" she asked quietly.

He hesitated, then sighed. "My wife."

"And she's dead?" B.J. prompted.

"Yes, she died in a plane crash two years ago."

"I'm so sorry."

"You're sorry? You don't know the meaning of the word." He looked at her briefly, then looked away. "I'm the one who's sorry. She wouldn't have been on that plane if I hadn't practically ordered her to fly to Saudi where I was working." The dam broke, and he was drowning in words. "We had bought the new house in Tampa and in two years Jared would have been starting kindergarten."

"Your son?" she asked in surprise.

He nodded. "This was the last job they could be with me, and I insisted they come. I even bought the tickets for that flight. I had a part in their deaths as much as if I'd planted the bomb that blew up their plane."

Bomb? Two years ago. It had been on all the news channels. A Middle Eastern terrorist group had taken revenge on another country for holding their leader hostage. There had been no survivors.

"This week they tried the men who planned the bombing. I had to watch the films and see the wreckage. I had to testify to my senseless loss, but I don't hate those men any more than I hate myself."

"You couldn't have known, Dana. It wasn't your fault." She thought of her false assumptions about his week in court. "I'm so sorry I thought and said the things I did. I didn't know. I'm so very sorry."

He looked at her and shook his head. "So now you know, but I don't want your pity. And I couldn't live with your mistrust. Let's just leave things the way they are."

She rose stiffly, knowing she had been dismissed. "If you're okay now, I'll just say good night."

"Good night. And thanks. I'll try not to disturb you again."

B.J. did not go to sleep until just before dawn and did not hear Dana when he left for the plant with Pete Marshall. She had intended to ask him about changing shifts with her but after all that happened, decided to wait until the next week.

She had cleaned the villa, done laundry, and shopped for groceries yesterday in preparation for Dana's arrival. Today time hung heavy on her hands. Since she had the use of the Escort, she decided to drive to Frederiksted and spend a few hours shopping.

Wandering aimlessly through an elite dress shop, B.J. observed that prices were obviously aimed at fleecing the wealthy tourists who visited the island. She stopped to admire a filmy dress in the variegated shades of the Caribbean.

"Would look so preteee on you, miss," the salesclerk told her. "You try eet on?"

Well, why not, she asked herself, then nodded.

The dress did become her, she had to admit. The price tag was obscene by her economical standards, but then she remembered that she didn't have to justify her spending to Tom Sutherland anymore, so she bought it. The new dress required a paler turquoise slip, and she couldn't resist the matching bra and panties. While she was on a roll, she splurged on a dainty white pelisse nightgown. Lugging her purchases to the car, B.J. silently questioned her behavior. Why on earth had she done it? She had no place to wear a dress like that and certainly no need to sleep in such a feminine nightie. She earned plenty of money to indulge herself, she answered, so why not?

B.J. treated herself to lunch in the dining room of the elegant Fredrik Hotel, then drove back to the villa for a nap before starting her midnight shifts. All day she had managed to avoid thinking about Dana and last night, but now as she tried to sleep, all that happened was replayed in her mind, and she was powerless to stop it. The night and perhaps even her future could have turned out much differently if she hadn't spelled out all her misconceptions about him. She had insulted him with her suspicions and he wasn't going to give her a second chance to trust him. After what he'd been through, who could blame him? Finally, a troubled sleep blotted out her useless regrets.

CHAPTER EIGHT

B.J. approached the control room with apprehension. It was going to be hard to face Dana for the first time after last night. With Frank Kelly and Pete Marshall looking on, she hoped she wouldn't reveal her true feelings for him. Luckily, with the shift change taking place, there were four operators as well as the same number of trainees present, so her conversation with Dana went unnoticed in the crowded room.

Dana stood when she walked toward the control panel, and she took the chair he'd vacated and scanned the board.

"I've taken all the readings, Sutherland," he said, not looking at her. "All's well."

"Okay," she answered, eyes still focused on the indicators. Then she frowned. "Isn't this setpoint on the ID fans too high?"

He glanced over her shoulder, irked by her contradiction. "I don't believe so."

"Just the same, I think I'll have Lohr go out and check the slag screen to be sure."

"That's not necessary," Dana told her curtly as he turned to go.

"Well, pardon my suspicious attitude," B.J. said softly.

"Par for the course, Sutherland," Dana said and kept on walking toward the door.

She glared at his receding back. He wasn't going to forgive her, and he wasn't going to let her forget it. This job couldn't end too soon. It wasn't enough to have to do daily battle with that sexist Frank Kelly, now she would have to contend with Dana Thomas' comments about her poor judgment. The only difference was she abhorred Frank and God help her, she loved Dana.

It was a long night and B.J. drank strong black coffee to help her stay alert. Frank Kelly had left Desmond in charge of the other unit quite a while ago, and she suspected he was taking a nap in his car while the trainee worked in his place. She resented having to supervise both Desmond and Lohr, but from her past job experience knew that she was expected to work twice as hard as any male employee just to prove her worth. She could write a book on equal work for equal pay, but it wouldn't change the way things were.

She had kept a watch on the furnace draft all night. Lohr had reported the slag screen to be okay, but something wasn't right, though she couldn't put her finger on it. If Kelly would get back in the control room where he belonged, she'd take a walk out to the ID fans and check the inlet damper operators.

"Want to get a little shut-eye, Miss Sutherland?" Frank Kelly's mouth brushed B.J.'s ear as he bent and spoke to her in a low voice.

Startled, she swiveled her chair around and glared at him. "No, thanks, but I would like to check out the ID fans if you've finished."

His face flared red and without answering, he continued on to the other operator trainee's position at the board.

B.J. put on her hard hat and left the air-conditioned control room. The temperature in the hallway hit her like a hot blast from a furnace. Stepping outside the building, the heat and humidity of the tropical night seemed cool by comparison.

Reaching the equipment in question, she tried to turn the handle on the blow down valve on the air line. At first, it didn't move, so she applied more pressure and moisture blew out in a hissing stream.

"So, this may be part of the problem," she said to herself. That ought to show Dana Thomas that her suspicious nature might sometimes come in handy in averting trouble. She would get back to the control room and write a work order for maintenance to check it out first thing in the morning, and she would have the satisfaction of entering this information in the log book. It would be hard not to add an "I told you so" in the margin.

B.J. was sleeping soundly when she became aware of the phone's incessant ringing. She opened her eyes and squinted at the bedside clock. Only eleven. She forced herself to get up and answer the phone which seemed determined to ring forever if she didn't.

"Hello?" Her voice was barely a whisper. She cleared her throat and tried again, louder. "Hello?" This had better be good to wake her after three hours sleep.

"Betty Jo? Hi, it's Racine."

"Hi." She made an effort to sound pleased. "How are you?"

"Bored to tears with Atlanta. How are you?"

"Sleepy. I just worked my first midnight shift."

"Oh, sweetie, I hope I didn't wake you?" She didn't wait for an answer. "But I just had to tell you this marvelous idea I've had. Mother spent all weekend talking about how beautiful the island is. She says you have twin beds in your room, so I thought I'd just hop on over and see for myself."

B.J. groaned inwardly. She might have known. Her mother had had just about enough time to plan her next strategy. It was obvious she thought her little girl's situation needed a second opinion and who better than her eldest daughter to give one?

When she didn't immediately respond, Racine continued. "You won't have to go to any trouble for me. I'll just amuse myself at the pool while you're sleeping. And it will only be for the weekend since I've already used all of my vacation time at the bank for this year."

Racine worked at the same bank where their father had been an investment counselor until his retirement. She sat at a desk in the front lobby. Her main task was to look pretty and smile at all the customers, which suited her skills just right.

"I'm working twelve hour shifts, Racine. I'll scarcely be able to see you."

"No problem. Anyway, Mother says you have a housemate, so maybe I could hang out with her in the evenings."

"Well, you see—" B.J. began, then thought better of trying to explain Dana Thomas over the phone. She would have to tell Racine, but it would be better to do it after her sister saw the situation for herself.

"I can't wait to see you, and I am dying to do some shopping after what Mother told me about shops in Christiansted."

B.J. knew when she was defeated. She accepted the inevitable with as much grace as she could muster at the moment. "When will you be arriving?"

"Oh, I booked the earliest flight possible—tentatively, of course—so you wouldn't have to stay up late to meet me. I'll get there at eight Saturday morning."

"Okay. I'll be waiting at the airport. Have a safe trip."

"Great. See you there. Bye."

B.J. stood holding the dead phone, hoping she had just awakened from a nightmare and none of the conversation had really happened. How on earth was she going to manage her sister's visit with the strained relations that now existed between her and Dana Thomas? What would he say when she told him about her weekend visitor? She owed it to him to let him know right away. Perhaps he would choose to bunk in with the men in one of the other villas while Racine was here. No, after he got one look at her glamorous sister he would be more likely to invite her to share his room.

Putting the phone in its cradle, B.J. trudged back to bed. She needed sleep. Her nerves were already on edge from all the coffee she'd consumed to stay awake last night. She couldn't afford to sleep on the job as her fellow operator had done. That would give ChemCorp a reason to accuse her of not being capable of doing shift work because she was a woman.

B.J. knew that she would have little opportunity to break the news of her sister's impending visit to her house-mate except at shift change, and she decided the sooner done, the better. As she relieved Dana that evening she planned to tell him but before she could open her mouth to begin, he spoke first.

"I thought you checked the setting on the furnace draft regulator last night, Sutherland." He swiveled around in his chair and stood.

"I did. It was okay after I blew the moisture out of the air lines." She remained standing, and they faced each other in the crowded room, close enough to touch. "Is there a problem?"

"Only if you call having to operate with ID inlet dampers

on manual all morning a problem," he told her facetiously.

"I made a note of my findings in the log and submitted a work order to maintenance to inspect the air dryer. Didn't they do it?" She looked puzzled.

"This is the first word I've heard about a work order."

"Well, didn't you read the log?" she said, raising her voice to be heard above the noise of the other conversations.

He ignored the question. "There was no work order here. Are you sure you wrote one?"

"Are you accusing me of ignorance or carelessness?" she asked evenly.

"I'm not accusing you of anything, Sutherland. But facts are facts, and we had a furnace draft problem that could have been avoided with a little more attention to details."

"It happened on your shift, Thomas, not mine." She seated herself at the board and gave her attention to the control panel, motioning for her trainee to join her.

"But it didn't start then," he said emphatically as he turned to leave.

"Oh, one other small detail I almost overlooked," B.J. swung around to face his receding back. "I have a visitor coming this weekend. If you don't mind?"

He stopped, turned. "Visitor?"

"Yes, my sister Racine."

"Fine with me."

"She's under the mistaken notion you're a woman, and she's expecting you to keep her company while I'm working."

"You didn't tell your parents then?"

Lohr looked on with ill-concealed amusement at the exchange going on between the operators.

"I saw no reason to."

"But you'll have to tell your sister. I'm damn well not going to dress in drag just to uphold your virtue."

Lohr had a sudden fit of coughing and covered his mouth.

"Nobody asked you to." She glared at Dana and then Lohr.

The control room grew quieter with the day shift gone, and Frank Kelly left his position at the board and came to stand beside her chair.

"Marshall said they'd had an instrument air problem today."

"Marshall was right." She ignored him as she continued

to take readings and enter them in her log book.

"I understand you checked on that last night and thought you submitted a work order to get it checked." He made it sound like a question.

"Don't you start, Kelly. I've already had to justify my competence once and that's enough."

"My, my, aren't we touchy this evening. PMS?" He patted her shoulder and winked at Lohr.

"Could be." She gave him a false smile. "Mind if I borrow your car for a nap—after you of course."

Frank's face flushed scarlet, and he returned to his chair without a word. Good riddance. She'd had quite enough of arrogant males for one night. It was clear she was to be made the scapegoat for every problem that surfaced on this job. It didn't matter so much with Kelly and the others, but now Dana Thomas had joined them and that mattered more than she wanted to admit. With a sigh of resignation, B.J. turned her attention back to her log book.

She would soon be able to find her way to Alexander Hamilton Airport in her sleep, B.J. thought as she parked the Escort and went into the terminal waiting room. Sleep was just what she was in need of at the moment, but she knew there was little chance of getting any until her sister was settled into the villa.

At least when she'd called the terminal they had said the plane would be on time. With any luck, she could be in bed by noon. Dana had generously offered her the use of the car during the days Racine was here even though it was his turn to drive himself and Pete Marshall to work. Word had gotten around that her sister was coming, and Pete had offered to show her around in the evenings while she was at work. Frank Kelly had said he'd be willing to forego sleep to do likewise during the day while she slept. Of the eligible bachelors, only Dana Thomas had not volunteered to be her sister's escort, and she wasn't certain if she should be sorry or glad for that.

The 737 dropped out of the clouds and roared to a short

stop on the runway, and B.J. stood watching the passengers disembark. It wasn't difficult to spot her sister, who was a younger version of Matilda. With her leopard-figured halter dress and matching framed sun glasses there were few eyes that missed her grand entrance into the terminal, followed by a porter carrying her monogrammed Louis Vitton luggage. B.J. wished there had been time to shower and change clothes at the villa before coming to the airport.

Racine flashed a brilliant smile at the customs agent, and he waved her through with a flourish as though she was royalty.

"B.J., I'm here," Racine announced unnecessarily as she threw her arms around her younger sister, leaving a lingering scent of Chanel. With her three inch heels, she was almost as tall as her younger sister.

"Welcome to St. Croix," B.J. said sincerely as she tipped the porter and waved him on. She loved her sister and they had always had a warm relationship. It was just that they had nothing in common. B.J. had always enjoyed competing in sports while the only sport Racine had excelled at was flirting and her competition was limited to getting the most invitations to sorority dances.

"I am just so thrilled to be here. I had the most exciting flight. The pilot is going to call me when I get back to Atlanta. Can you believe he just walked right up and started talking to me at the airport before we boarded?"

"I can believe that," B.J. said wryly as she picked up the two bags and steered her sister toward the door. "What are you carrying in here? Feels like Styrofoam from the weight of it."

Racine giggled. "Actually, almost nothing. I plan to shop until I drop at those fabulous stores Mother told me about. They'll be much heavier when I go back."

"So you want to get started as soon as the shops open, don't you?" B.J. asked with resignation.

"Absolutely."

They exited the terminal and B.J. led the way toward the Escort.

"Oh, my, how do you endure this killing heat?" Racine asked. "It almost takes my breath away."

"You get accustomed to it," B.J. said. "And the trade wind blows."

On the drive to Christiansted, B.J. tried to find an opportune moment to tell her sister about her living arrangement with Dana Thomas, but she found it impossible to get a word in edgewise as Racine babbled on about her current divorce proceedings, interspersed with comments on the island scenery.

Once they reached the villa the matter had to be addressed. B.J. parked the Ford and prepared to face the music.

"What a picturesque setting," Racine exclaimed as B.J. unlocked the patio gate. "It would make an absolutely romantic hideaway."

"It's quite comfortable. I had to make do with a motel on the Minnesota job." B.J.'s reply gave no indication that her sister's first impression of the villa had been the same as her own. She opened the door and led the way inside.

"I love it." Racine did a complete turn as she admired the furnished room. "It's so...so tropical. All it needs is Brad Pitt to complete it."

B.J. smiled grimly. She would never have a better opening than now. "Well, there is a man living here, but I'm afraid he isn't Brad."

"Oh, what fun!" Racine squealed. "Mother was right then. She said she was sure you were involved with a man."

"I'm *not* involved with anyone," B.J. protested. "Chemcorp rented villas which had to be shared. Since I'm the only woman on the job, I have a male house-mate."

" He's married? Mother thought he was but—"

"No, Dana Thomas lost his wife and son in a plane crash."

"Oh the poor darling." Racine was quiet a moment, absorbing this new information. "I guess that makes the setup perfect for you, doesn't it?"

"Yes, it does," B.J. said decisively. "He's not interested in fun and games, and neither am I."

"Betty Jo, you have been divorced from Tom Sutherland for four years, and you haven't given any man a second glance. It's time you looked for another husband."

"Like you did?" B.J. lifted her eyebrows meaningfully.

"So I made the same mistake twice." Racine shrugged her shapely shoulders. "Can I help it if I'm attracted to losers?"

"Sorry," B.J. touched her sister's arm. "That was a low blow."

"But right on," Racine countered. "Next time I'm going to look for a different kind of guy. Someone not so...so..."

"Preppy?" B.J. suggested.

"Right. No more university grads from Atlanta's best families. I'm going after a rugged kind of guy, someone who works for a living. Handsome and clever and sensitive, of course."

B.J. felt a sinking sensation in the pit of her stomach. Her sister had just described Dana Thomas and made her intentions perfectly clear. All she had to do now was meet him, and she would know fate had sent her Mister Right. She reached for the luggage. "Come on, my bedroom is this way."

"I'll unpack later," Racine said as she followed. "I want to start shopping first. I need a new bikini, and I thought I'd wait and buy one here, something definitely daring."

It would be like watching a mouse drawn to a baited trap. B.J. groaned inwardly. Dana Thomas would never know what lured him until he felt the spring snap on his unsuspecting neck.

After brunch of French toast with bananas and whipped cream at Antoine's, the two sisters canvassed the shops until mid-afternoon. In spite of her two cups of espresso, B.J. was beginning to feel like a sleep walker by the time Racine had made her purchases. There wasn't time enough left to have lunch at the Buccaneer and B.J. get a nap before work, so they had quiche and lime drinks at a sidewalk cafe and drove back to the villa.

"I'll just slather myself with sunscreen and hang out at the pool while you're sleeping," Racine said as she dumped her packages onto the spare twin bed and began searching for her new leopard skin bikini.

B.J. yawned. "I'll leave my keys with you, just in case Dana isn't here when you come in." She shrugged off her jeans and headed for the bathroom, hoping with all her heart he wouldn't be. A hot shower and a cool bed were going to be heaven. Then she thought of Racine returning to the villa in her next-to-nothing bikini after her house-mate came home and a far-from-heavenly expression came to mind. Her sister seemed to have a penchant for leopards these days which probably made a statement about being on the prowl. Perhaps Dana would go out with some of the other guys and give Racine some privacy as he had done for her when they had first shared the villa. It was too much to hope for. Dana Thomas was a marked man.

"You'll be sure to call me if the lady wants an escort for the evening," Pete reminded Dana as he got out of the car.

"Right." He walked toward the gate, digging his keys out of his pocket. The villa was dark making him wonder if the lady had already gone out. It was a nuisance having her here but what could he say? B.J. hadn't sounded exactly thrilled about the visit either, so he supposed it hadn't been her idea. Well, it was only for the weekend, and he could always call Pete.

Letting himself in, Dana switched on the lights and went to take a shower. The stall was still steamy. He closed his eyes and imagined B.J. standing under the warm water in nothing but her bronzed skin. Better not to let his imagination run wild like that. Besides, it could have been her sister in the shower for all he knew.

He dressed again in jeans in deference to the house guest who was probably as uptight as B.J. had been about wearing the proper at-home attire. Dana knew it would have been sensible to go out for the evening, alone, and leave the mystery woman to her own devices but some perverse feeling of being imposed on by her presence caused him to stay.

There was no sign of any action in the kitchen. He guessed that their guest probably ate health food the way B.J. did. He opened a beer and made a double-decker ham, cheese, and turkey sandwich then sat down at the snack bar to eat.

"Hi there."

He hadn't heard anyone come in, and he jerked his head around at the sound of the honey-coated southern drawl, almost toppling from the bar stool. What he saw crossing the room toward him was nearly enough to finish the job.

The woman was petite and wearing an x-rated swim suit that showed all her assets to the max. Her silken blond hair was piled on top of her head, and she flashed him a smile that said blondes really did have more fun.

"Hello, you must be..." He trailed off as he stood.

"Betty Jo's sister," she finished for him. She held out her hand, and he took it, breathing in the heady scent she wore. "And you're—"

"Dana Thomas," they finished together and laughed.

"Have a good swim?" he asked as she still held onto his hand.

"Yes, wonderful. This place is paradise." She sighed and slowly let go of him. "All those heavenly shops."

"Oh, you've been in Christiansted already?" He thought of B.J. probably staying up all day to take her sister shopping.

"Most of the day. I just couldn't tear myself away from all those lovely things to buy. I only have two days, you know." She smiled at him again and added, "This time."

No wonder B.J. had looked so pale this evening when she had relieved him. She had scarcely spoken two words to him and fairly bit his head off when he'd asked if her sister had gotten in all right.

"Mmmm, that looks good." She stepped closer and motioned to his sandwich. "What are you having?"

He told her and then asked, "Want one? There's plenty."

"I'd love it. I'm starved." She wriggled onto the other stool. "I'd like a Coors, too, if you don't mind."

"Sure." Was this woman who looked like a stripper and ate and drank like a man really B.J. Sutherland's sister? He turned toward the refrigerator and took out what he needed and put together another club sandwich. Apparently this one had a hang-up about doing kitchen work, too. He gave her the plate and a frosty beer then sat down again.

She had a hearty appetite and drank her beer from the bottle like she had done it before. He studied her from the corner of his eye. She was nothing like B.J. but then, he'd never met another woman like B.J. and that was part of what attracted him.

"Ummm, delicious." She smiled at him as she licked a crumb from her lip with a seductively slow movement.

"Want another?" he asked with amusement as he finished his own sandwich and washed it down with the last of his beer.

"Thanks, but I couldn't eat another bite." She slid off the stool in slow motion. "I would like to take a shower, if you've finished with the bathroom?"

"Sure. Go right ahead."

"I don't suppose..." She shook her head. "No, never mind."

"What?" He stopped midway to the dishwasher and turned to look at her.

"Well," she made it a three syllable word, "I was just wondering what you all did for fun around here at night?"

"Oh, there's plenty of entertainment at the hotels and clubs. Lots of good bands for dancing."

She gave a wistful sigh. "I wish Betty Jo had her evenings free this weekend. I would have loved to go out on the town."

It was obvious where this was leading and the next move was up to him. He felt a sense of responsibility toward B.J.'s sister and couldn't in good conscience throw her to the wolves, or wolf as Pete Marshall was the only other single man free this evening. He took a deep breath. "Since your sister is working, would you like me to fill in for her?"

"Why, that would be so sweet, if you're sure it wouldn't be an imposition?"

"I'd be happy to," he assured her, then glanced at his watch. "We'd better get going as soon as you're ready. Weekends are crowded at the Cormorant Beach Club, and we don't have a reservation."

"I won't be a sec," she promised and hurried toward the bedroom.

Dana contemplated his offer as he loaded the dishwasher. Maybe he ought to have called Pete after all. He really didn't look forward to spending an evening being pummeled by a bunch of happy drunks on a dance floor but what choice had he?

"Excuse me?" Racine was standing close behind him. "I just can't fasten this chain, and I know we're in a hurry..."

She held out the slender gold chain to him, then turned away, her long hair flowing about her shoulders creating a slight breeze that renewed his awareness of that same sultry fragrance. She was wearing a blue sarong-type dress dotted with splashes of vivid color which contrasted sharply with her bare back. Dana sucked in his breath. Maybe the evening wasn't going to be so bad after all.

CHAPTER NINE

B.J. had a miserable night. There had been no further problems with the ID fans, and Frank Kelly had steered clear of her after their encounter early in the shift. He even remained on the job except to take a break for dinner. Even so, it had been difficult to concentrate on operating procedures when her head was filled with images of her glamorous sister and Dana alone in the villa.

It was obvious that the man was still vulnerable because of the loss he had suffered, and Racine was on the rebound from her last disastrous marriage. It was a situation made for fireworks and if she knew her sister, Racine would be only too willing to light the fuse. But what was that to her? Dana had refused to accept her apology for reaching the wrong conclusion about him, had made it clear he wasn't willing to give her another chance to trust him. He'd even jumped on the popular band wagon that blamed B.J. Sutherland for everything that went wrong at the job site.

She glanced at the wall clock that hung over the control panel. Dana and Pete should be getting here soon. Maybe she would be able to get a few hours of sleep before Racine woke up and began her sightseeing trek around the island.

Dana paused for a minute at the plant entrance as Pete

Marshall went ahead. The man was ticked off with him after learning that he had taken B.J.'s sister to the Cormorant last night without asking him to come along. How could he explain to anyone that it had been an obligation to B.J. that had led him to stay up half the night dancing to calypso music?

All the while he had been remembering a few days earlier when he had danced with B.J. on that terrace and how good she felt in his arms. That had been a night ripe with tantalizing expectations that turned sour before he could taste them, and they had snarled at each other ever since.

He blamed his repressed libido for the way he had behaved over the matter of the ID fans. It had been unfair to ignore her concern and then accuse her of carelessness. He ought to apologize for that.

Dana stepped quietly into the noisy control room and motioned for his trainee to take over the control board, then bent to speak to B.J. in a low voice. "I'd like a word with you. I'll wait in the hallway."

She nodded and followed him out.

Dana walked to the far end of the hallway and stopped beside a water fountain, well out of the path of the men who would be leaving. The woman who faced him was pale and had dark smudges under her lovely blue-green eyes. He felt a rush of tenderness for her and wanted nothing more than to take her in his arms and smooth away her fatigue. Or better still, take her back to the villa and tuck her into bed.

"Well?" she asked, and he realized he had been standing there for some minutes lost in his fantasies.

"I owe you an apology."

"Oh?"

She wasn't going to make this easy. "I shouldn't have insinuated that you forgot to leave a work order yesterday, and I should have acknowledged that the setpoint on the ID fans was high when you caught that, but I thought you were just nitpicking. I'm sorry."

"Accepted." She looked at him intently. "Did you meet my sister?"

"Yes, we met." He took a deep breath. He might as well get this over with before she heard it from Racine. "I...took her to the Cormorant, as a matter of fact."

"You and Pete?" she asked in a neutral voice.

"No, just me. I didn't want..." He stopped, unable to decide how to explain that he had done it for her, to keep her ditsy sister out of trouble.

"Any competition?" she asked with a smile that didn't quite reach her eyes.

"No, that wasn't the reason I—" he began but she cut him off.

"You don't have to explain anything to me. I'm not my sister's keeper, and what you do is certainly no concern of mine."

"It could have been," he told her quietly.

"Yes, well, lucky for both of us that didn't work out or you might not have a clear playing field with my sister."

"Who said I wanted one? There you go again, jumping to your fast conclusions without a shred of evidence."

"No evidence?" She looked incredulous. "You spend the night with my sister and then have the nerve to say—"

"Spend the night with your sister? Now wait a—"

"In a manner of speaking, Thomas. At least I have no proof that you literally—"

"Oh, there you are, Miss Sutherland." Frank Kelly stood a few feet behind them. "I hope I'm not interrupting anything important, but I wondered if you're ready to leave now? I'm expecting a phone call at the villa in a short while."

"No, you're not, Kelly, and yes, I'm ready." With a final glare at Dana, she added in a low voice, "This conversation is over."

Dana stood watching as B.J. walked toward Kelly. He should have known she'd misinterpret his sincere attempt to be nice to her sister. Her reaction almost made him believe she was jealous. If she only knew how little he was attracted to a woman like Racine she'd have no reason to be. His head ached from too much rum and too little sleep. This run-in with B.J. had made his day complete. With an injured sigh, he turned toward the control room to face a busy morning.

B.J. entered the villa as quietly as possible so as not to disturb her sister, whom she hoped would sleep late. What she saw in the living room stopped her in her tracks. A pair of gold evening slippers with spike heels was in the middle of the floor and a matching clutch bag lay on the sofa. Two stemmed glasses, partly filled with wine, stood on the coffee table in front of it, and the scent of Chanel still lingered like a ghost at the seduction scene.

With pressed lips, she crossed to the snack bar and threw down her back pack. She jerked open the refrigerator, pulled out a can of juice, and downed it. What had she expected? That her sister would behave like a nun and ignore the most gorgeous man alive once she'd seen him? Fat chance of that. He was made to order for Husband Number Three. Racine must have realized that right away and lost no time in launching her campaign to convince him. Not that Dana Thomas would need much convincing, she added bitterly.

He'd probably been all too eager to escort the glamorous Ms. Lindsey out for a night on the town. To take her to the Cormorant of all places, the place where they had been just days ago was like a slap in the face. She could see it now; Dana and her sister dancing on the shadowed terrace with a tropical moon turning the dark Caribbean to silver.

B.J. was at least mollified to find Racine sprawled in one of the twin beds in her room instead of across the hall, but her skimpy sarong puddled on the floor was further evidence of what had taken place. Shedding her clothes, B.J. tip-toed to the shower where she found Racine's black teddy draped over the tub. Perhaps they'd shared a bubble bath together. She turned the shower on full force but it did little to soothe her roiling emotions. If Racine wasn't her sister, she'd send her packing right now.

A pleasant aroma of brewing coffee woke B.J., and she slowly opened one eye. She squinted to read the lighted dial of her bedside clock in the darkened room to find it was after one. She threw back the covers and reached for her terry cloth robe, then remembered that Dana wasn't in the villa and went to the kitchen in her long faded tee shirt.

The sight of her sister in a silk wrap-around with a vibrant Chinese dragon design reminded her that Racine most definitely was here and of what had happened last night. Hearing B.J. come in, Racine turned and gave her a brilliant smile.

"Good morning." She laughed softly. "Actually, it's afternoon. I slept what was left of the morning."

"Mmmm." Not trusting herself to say more, B.J. reached for a cup and filled it from the coffee-maker.

"I had the most marvelous time last night," Racine went on, ignoring B.J.'s lack of enthusiasm. "Dana took me to the Cormorant Beach Club, and we danced the night away. He dances divinely."

B.J. sipped her coffee in silence.

"I thought you said he wasn't interested in fun and games? He kept me laughing all evening with his stories of places he's been and things he's done." She climbed onto a stool at the counter and crossed a shapely leg.

"I haven't seen that side of him," B.J. admitted dourly, then changed the subject. "If you don't have anything special in mind, I thought we'd go to the Buccaneer for lunch today. I'll call Albert Zurow and ask if I can report to work a little later tonight, so I can take you to the airport."

"Oh, that won't be necessary, Betty Jo. Dana has already invited me to dinner at the Buccaneer and plans to wait with me until my flight leaves. I'd rather go shopping again, maybe in Frederiksted?"

B.J. sighed and stared into the depths of her cup. "Sounds like you've got all the bases covered then." *And I just struck out*, she added silently.

"I'm definitely going to come back before you finish this job, but next time I'll come when you're working days. Dana has offered to teach me to play golf."

"Golf? Dad could teach you to play golf. Or I could. You've always hated golf!" She looked at her sister in amazement.

Racine smiled slyly. "Well, maybe I just never had a reason to like it before."

B.J. put her cup on the counter with a loud thud. "I'll get dressed now."

"Betty Jo?"

Racine's voice stopped her halfway to the bedroom, and she turned.

"Is that the only nightie you have to wear?"

Remembering the frilly nightgown she had bought on a whim in Frederiksted, B.J. didn't answer but asked a question of her own instead. "What's wrong with it?"

Racine's eyes swept the faded, over-sized garment with speculation. "Nothing, if you're one of the guys, but it might explain why Dana Thomas wasn't interested in fun and games."

"Could be," B.J. readily agreed, "but like I told you, I'm not interested in that either. Dana and I are house-mates by necessity, and we have a working relationship. That's the way we both want it."

Racine looked thoughtfully after her sister as she walked toward the bedroom. "I wonder," she mused softly. "To quote the Bard, Methinks thou doth protest too much."

Since Frank Kelly had taken sick leave and Pete Marshall was doubling over, B.J. drove to work alone. She was going in early to give Dana plenty of time to wine and dine her sister in style before she caught her plane although the thought of them spending any time together hurt like a migraine headache.

Racine had been wearing a clingy blue dress that exactly matched her baby-blue eyes, and B.J. could just imagine Dana's reaction when he saw her. They would make a striking couple. Dana was tall, dark, and handsome while Racine was petite, blond, and beautiful. Then a sudden cold panic gripped her middle section. Dana Thomas might end up her brother-in-law! How on earth would she be able to cope with that? It was bad enough to love him and lose him, but to lose him to her sister Racine and have him become a permanent member of the family would be unbearable. She'd have to apply for overseas work until her retirement just to avoid seeing him.

Still in a resentful frame of mind, B.J. parked the car and made her way to the control room. She went to stand beside Dana's chair and when he became aware of her presence, he glanced quickly at the wall clock.

"I came in early," she said unnecessarily, "so you could have more time for your date."

"You didn't need to do that," he told her, then grinned. "But as long as you're here, I may as well leave."

He stood and she sat in his vacated chair. "Everything okay here?" B.J. was business-as-usual although she felt close to tears. Why did he have to affect her this way?

"Maintenance has reported a bad conductivity reading on a feedwater sample, but I checked the setting on the chemical feed pumps and everything looked okay."

"I'll do another check later then." She wished he'd stop looking at her that way and just go. "Thanks for taking my sister to the airport, and to dinner tonight."

He shrugged. "You're welcome. It's my pleasure."

I'll just bet it is, she said silently, not knowing who to be most angry with, Dana or Racine.

He hesitated. "Well, I'll be going now."

She gritted her teeth. "Enjoy your evening."

"I wish you could go with us." He looked sincere when he said it, but she wasn't fooled.

"And pigs fly," she mumbled.

"Excuse me?" he asked.

"I said goodbye," she answered shortly and turned toward the control board with an exaggerated frown of concentration.

Dana watched her for a moment, wondering if she had on her scarlet undies beneath her chaste white shirt and jeans. Then he became aware of the two trainees watching him and hastily made his retreat.

He thought about B.J. all the way to the villa, wondering if her surly attitude had anything to do with him taking her sister out last night. Racine Lindsey was not the type of woman who took no for an answer, so he really hadn't had a lot of choice in the matter without being downright rude. Besides, she was B.J.'s sister. He couldn't in good conscience send her out on the town alone or with Pete Marshall, and he had only offered to take her to the airport tonight as a favor to B.J. It had been Racine's idea to go to the Buccaneer for dinner beforehand.

One positive thing had come out of it, though. He had learned more about B.J. He now knew that she had been married for ten years, and that her husband worked for IPPS. Though he still didn't understand why she wanted to work for the same company, or even why she wanted to be a power plant operator. Racine didn't seem to know the answers either or else she wasn't telling him.

Of course, Racine had preferred talking about her own two failed marriages and how she was looking for a real man to love. He'd gotten her message loud and clear. Someone like him, but he wasn't interested. He'd let her know that when they got back to the villa last night, and she'd come on to him. Even that slinky dress she'd worn hadn't turned him on like B.J.'s plain shirts and jeans. The black lace nightie she'd left in the bathroom didn't excite his fantasies as much as B.J.'s faded sleep shirt either.

It was B.J. he loved, and B.J. he wanted. He knew this, but he was wary of committing himself to anyone without a mutual trust. Even though he knew B.J.'s husband had betrayed her big time, it shouldn't mean she'd never trust again.

The lights of the villa glowed just ahead, and he resigned himself to one more evening of Racine's frivolous chatter when he'd rather be talking turbines with B.J.

When they arrived, the Buccaneer was crowded with weekend tourists. They had to wait for a table even though Dana had called in a reservation. He was dressed in his best chinos and white knit shirt, which was the nearest thing to formal wear he had brought to the island. Racine had assured him he looked great. It went without saying that she was a knockout in that blue dress she was wearing, but he complimented her anyway, even though he preferred B.J.'s simple skirt and top she'd worn to the airport to meet him that day.

Finally seated, they ordered prime rib and lobster. They were soon served their wine and salad. The slight breeze brought by the trade wind was scented with jasmine and oleander which mingled with the now-familiar fragrance Racine wore. The soft melodious rhythm of a steel drum throbbed from the bar and shadowy figures kept time with the beat.

"This is so lovely," Racine's eyes swept the terrace and the dark Caribbean beyond. "Thank you for bringing me here."

"My pleasure," Dana told her and added silently, *to do this for your sister.*

"Betty Jo is a very lucky girl, sharing a villa in this tropical

paradise with a man like you." Her eyes glowed with admiration, and he wondered with some trepidation where this was
leading.

"Dana," Racine put down her glass and looked at him, "I
want to ask you a question. A very personal question, if you
don't mind?"

He already knew from past experience with her sister
that she would ask it anyway. "Okay."

"We talked last night about your wife but I'd like to
know...do you still love her?"

"Yes, I still love her," he answered without hesitation.
"But I'm not in love with Kate now."

"Then you are ready for a new relationship with someone
else?" she persisted.

Hadn't he made it clear to Racine last night that he was-
n't interested in her? Was he going to have to spell it out in
plain language that would prove embarrassing to them both?
"I could be, with the right person."

"Dana," she waited until he met her eyes, "Are you in
love with Betty Jo?"

"Yes," he blurted out truthfully. The question was so unexpected that Dana didn't even have time to deny it. Even if
he'd tried, his emotions must be written plainly across his
face. "How did you know?" How was it that the woman he
loved could be oblivious to his feelings, but her sister easily
saw right through him?

She smiled. "Not too many men turn me down, and nobody turns down something for nothing."

"Nothing is exactly what I've got," he admitted ruefully.

"Whose fault is that?" she chided, "Have you told my sister how you feel?"

"I've tried to, but she laid out the rules about a fling..
Every time I try to tell her how I really feel, I swear I only
mess things up more. As soon as the word fling was out
there, I think I lost any chance at her opening up to me."

"Well, I can't blame her for that," Racine said indignantly.
"No woman would want to be just a one-night stand with a
guy like you."

"You've got it all wrong. It wasn't me who wanted the
fast fling. She did."

"Unbelievable." Racine shook her head. "She was only
trying to protect herself from getting hurt again. Trust me.

That isn't what she really wants."

"She could have fooled me."

"Listen, if you love her, tell her. The rest will take care of itself." She reached out and patted his arm reassuringly. "Be sure to invite me to the wedding."

"You have my word on that," he said, still not daring to believe her simplistic solution to his dilemma.

The waiter brought their dinner and while he was placing it on the table, Racine said with a conspiratorial smile, "And Dana?"

"Yes?"

"I really hate golf, but my sister loves it."

"I know." Dana grinned. "She's already beaten the socks off me."

Racine frowned. "I'll have to speak to her about that."

Feeling somewhat hopeful for the first time in days, Dana tackled his food with enthusiasm. His favor to B.J. just might turn out to benefit him most of all.

CHAPTER TEN

B.J. checked the clock with a worried frown. She had re-lieved Dana almost an hour early last night. Common cour-tesy dictated that he return the favor this morning, but there was no sign of him yet. Maybe he'd gotten on the plane with Racine, and they'd eloped. More likely he was having trouble getting his rear in gear this morning after his last tete-a-tete with her traitorous sister. Despite her annoyance at Dana, she had more pressing matters at the moment than the state of her love life.

She had called Albert Zurow, and he was on his way. She wanted to be back out in the plant when he arrived. He had sounded cross as a bear when she told him what happened, and she hoped he would have calmed down by the time he'd had his coffee and driven in. Why, oh why, did this have to happen on her shift?

"Good morning."

She swiveled quickly in her chair to see a smiling Dana Thomas standing behind her. He looked wonderful, and she felt a warm glow begin deep inside her that flowed to the surface of her skin, suffusing her face with color. "There's nothing good about it," she said shortly. "I've lost power on one feed pump, and we're running at half load."

Dana glanced at the other operator's chair where Des-mond sat at the controls. "Where's Kelly? Is he out there now?"

"Kelly is probably in bed. He took sick leave last night."

"Did Marshall double over?"

"Till after midnight," she explained. "Then he was feeling sick, too, so he left."

"And you've had it all by yourself? Why didn't you call me to come in?" he asked sharply.

She shrugged. "With the two trainees here, I thought it unnecessary, until the pump seized up."

"Has anyone checked it?" he demanded.

"I checked it," she shot back. "The bearing got hot and caused the shaft to snap in two."

He groaned softly. "That's big trouble."

"Don't you think I know that?" Her face registered both anger and apprehension.

"I'll go out and take a look at it." He started toward the door.

"Lohr, take over here," she told the other trainee in the control room, then said to Dana's receding back, "I'm coming with you."

She caught up with him in the hallway and matched his long strides to the pump area. There was no sign of Albert Zurow yet nor any of the maintenance crew.

Dana laid a hand on the bearing and quickly withdrew it. He looked at the broken shaft and shook his head.

"Wasn't anyone watching the temperature indicator?" His question sounded more like an accusation.

"I was watching it," she said furiously. "There was nothing, nothing I tell you, that was abnormal." She was near tears and fought to control her emotions. Operators didn't cry.

"You couldn't monitor everything at once," he insisted, "and I doubt very much if Desmond or Lohr would have noticed the problem until it was too late, especially when they were half asleep."

"I resent your implication that I didn't have the situation under control, Thomas." She glared at him. "Maybe you can only focus on one thing at a time, but I'm a woman, remember? It is the nature of women to be multi-focused."

He lifted an eyebrow. "As well as being unwilling to ask for help when it's clearly needed?"

"It was an accident. It could have happened on any shift. It..." A tear rolled down her cheek, and she angrily swiped at it with the back of her hand. "It just turned out to be ...m-mine." Another tear followed.

Dana reached out and gently brushed it away.

She looked at him quickly but her tears made his image waver. At first she thought it only an optical illusion that he was moving toward her. Then his mouth touched hers, igniting a spark that traveled to the tips of her steel-toed boots, and she knew it was no illusion.

The kiss was brief but his warm hands resting on her shoulders kept her standing close enough to feel the comforting strength of his body, "Yeah, you're right," he whispered. "Tough break, but it's not the end of the world."

"Excuse me?" Albert Zurow cleared his throat, and the two operators jumped apart. He looked sternly from one to the other and then pressed his lips in a thin, disapproving line.

"Any new developments since you called, Miss Sutherland?" he asked curtly. "With the pump, I mean."

"No, Mister Zurow," she answered contritely. "We were just checking the bearing, and it's still too hot to handle."

"Yes, the heat in here did not escape my attention," he said evenly.

Albert Zurow moved closer to the pump and examined its exterior. "I expect the whole thing will have to be replaced. We won't know for sure until we can get a look at the pump itself."

"I'm very sorry, Mister Zurow," B.J. told him sincerely, "but the temperature indicator appeared to be working properly, and there was absolutely no sign of any problem."

"So you said, Miss Sutherland." He looked at her sternly. "Why don't you go home now and get some sleep? Thomas and I will take it from here."

"Yes, sir." She hesitated, then asked. "How long before we're back to full load?"

He shrugged. "Two weeks, maybe longer if replacement of the pump is necessary. I'll have to contact the manufacturer to fly in a new one. We're a small plant, and we don't keep expensive spare equipment."

She nodded and walked away.

Dana watched regretfully as B.J. walked away. Now he'd

done it. Fraternizing among the troops was not approved of in IPPS. Not that the issue had come up before in his experience since this was his first job that had included a female operator. That must have made things worse for B.J. even without this cozy scene that Zurow had interrupted. He'd have to try and set things straight.

He cleared his throat. "Uh, Mister Zurow, that wasn't what it looked like back there a moment ago."

Zurow cocked his head and looked at Dana intently but didn't speak.

"B.J.—Miss Sutherland—was very upset about what happened, and she was trying to explain how it wasn't her fault. She broke down—"

"And appealed to you for sympathy?" Zurow smiled grimly.

"Actually, the offer of sympathy was my own idea. I guess considering the situation, I was out of line." He paused a moment, then added, "I would have sympathized with anyone under the circumstances."

" I would hope not in quite the same way, Thomas."

Zurow chuckled, and Dana realized that he had not convinced his boss of either B.J.'s innocence or his own good intentions.

"Point taken." He turned back toward the control room and Zurow walked with him.

"I've talked to the IPPS office in Miami, and they're sending a person over this afternoon." He paused outside the control room door. "I've expressed my concern about the way the job is going, and they've agreed to look into it."

"Anything in particular you're unhappy with?" Dana asked.

"There have been too many problems lately, and all of them on Miss Sutherland's shift. I've begun to wonder if having her on the job is such a good idea after all."

He walked away, leaving Dana with words of protest still unsaid. He swore silently. The woman had done as good a job as any man here. She'd put up with flack for being female besides, but Zurow would need a scapegoat for the decrease in production and it didn't take a second guess to figure out who that was going to be.

It was late afternoon when B.J. awoke from an exhausted sleep, punctuated intermittently by nightmares of overheated bearings and hot kisses that both spelled disaster. She lay in the semi-darkness of her bedroom, dreading to face Dana when he came back to the villa. There would be no avoiding it since her midnights were over and this was his last day shift. She would have to get through tonight and tomorrow with him before either went back to work.

The room was stifling, so she got up to open the shuttered windows to let in a breeze. Instead of the cool air she expected, there was only stillness and a strange eerie silence. B.J. peered into the dim light, then glanced at her clock, surprised to see that it was only six. They were surely in for a tropical storm, so she grabbed a robe and went to take a quick shower in case there was a power failure.

Putting on a pair of white shorts and yellow striped tee shirt, B.J. halved a small cantaloupe, scooped it out, then added cottage cheese and strawberries. She poured a glass of tea and sat down at the counter. In less than an hour Dana would be coming in, and she would learn the outcome of the day's events. She was anxious to know if the pump would have to be replaced as Albert Zurow predicted. Most of all, she wanted to know if he had commented further on what he had seen between her and Dana when he came into the plant this morning, though unless Dana mentioned it, she was reluctant to ask.

He might get the idea that she had read more into it than was meant, and she certainly hadn't. He had obviously been trying to help her get back in control of her emotions after her most unprofessional outburst, and she would have to explain that to Zurow when she had an opportunity.

B.J. became aware of a sound at the front of the villa and listened for a moment.

"Hello. Anybody in there?"

Could Dana have forgotten his keys? It didn't sound like his voice, she thought, as she hurried to open the door. In the dusk, she could see a man standing at the fence, impatiently rattling the gate. Panic gripped her for a moment before she recognized him.

"Tom?"

"Open the gate, Betty Jo," he commanded in the polished authoritative tone that she would recognize anywhere.

As she slowly came forward to do his bidding, she asked, "What are you doing here?"

"I could ask you the same thing," he said as he walked through the gate and confronted her in the courtyard. "Will you ask me in?"

"Uh, y-yes, of course," she stammered and walked through the door with him following. The room was dark except for the light above the snack bar, and she went about turning on lamps before she faced him. Why was he here? Did it have anything to do with what happened last night?

When she turned, he was standing in the middle of the room. He was wearing an expensive looking jacket that she would bet had a designer label, and she felt almost apologetic for her own informal attire.

"May I sit down?" he asked with a quizzical smile.

She flushed at her second faux pas in as many minutes which was par for the course. Her ex-husband had always had an uncanny knack of making her feel like an imbecile.

"Please do." She gestured toward the sofa and then asked before she could be caught in another glaring lapse of manners, "Coffee, tea?"

"Coffee, please."

B.J. nodded and went to fill the coffee maker. While it brewed, she remained in the kitchen, arranging two mugs, sugar and napkins on a tray. She glanced at her half-eaten food and wondered if she should offer to fix something for Tom but thought not.

"Nice place," Tom commented after a short silence.

"Yes, it's quite comfortable," she agreed.

A gust of wind rattled the blinds on the veranda. "Looks like we're in for a storm," Tom observed.

"Yes, it does," she answered as she placed the tray on the low table in front of him. It was obvious he wasn't about to reveal what had brought him to the island or to the villa until all the amenities had been satisfied. A true Southern aristocrat in every way, she said silently, except the one way that had really mattered.

He carefully measured two spoonfuls of sugar into his

coffee and looked at her. "May I have cream, please?"

"Sorry, I forgot that you use it." She tried to hide her smile of amusement at his irritation as she informed him there was only skimmed milk.

"How was the Minnesota job?" he asked as she brought the pitcher of milk.

"Cold." So he knew where she had worked.

"I meant," he stirred his coffee, not looking at her, "how did the job go?"

"Fine." Where was this leading?

"No problems? No equipment breakdowns?"

"Nothing out of the ordinary," she said evenly. "Look, Tom, my job performance report is on record if you want to read it. You didn't fly all the way to St. Croix just to ask me this, did you?"

"I flew over here because Albert Zurow called our office this morning raising havoc over the way IPPS start-up was going and threatened to cancel our contract. He said careless operating procedures had caused several equipment break-downs."

"I see." She put down her mug and clasped her hands together in her lap.

"This last fiasco will take at least two weeks to correct, maybe longer. That means the loss of big bucks to Chem-Corp."

"Then the pump has to be replaced, too?" she asked.

"Right, but it isn't the cost of equipment that Zurow is looking at. It's the loss of generation while the load is at fifty percent reduction that's going to be expensive. Can you understand that, Betty Jo?"

There was something in his condescending tone that made her see red. She took a deep breath and went on the offensive. "Contrary to your opinion of my IQ, Tom, I understand quite well. What I don't understand is why you are telling me this?"

"Because," he set his mug on the tray with a clatter, "Zurow says all the problems have occurred on equipment being monitored by one operator. The Miami office is of the opinion that the operator in question may need to be removed."

"I've done nothing wrong, Tom." Her voice rose against her will. "Unless you or someone else can prove otherwise, you have no grounds for taking me off this job!"

"There are other jobs, Betty Jo. You can transfer to the job is Texas or work in Miami until—"

"I don't want another job. I want to stay here at Chemcorp and prove that what's been happening is not my fault."

"I had hoped to persuade you otherwise." Tom shook his head sadly.

"Well, I'm afraid your powers of persuasion with me have lost their charm." She stood and wiped her hands on the sides of her shorts. "May I remind you, and you can take this little gem back with you to Miami, that I am female. I won't hesitate to file a discrimination suit if I have to."

"Are you making threats, Betty Jo?" Tom also stood and took a step toward her, "because if—"

The front door had been opened without a sound but the wind slammed it with a loud thud as Dana stood looking at the two people glaring at each other in the center of the living room.

Tom looked sharply at Dana, then turned an accusing eye on B.J. "Who is *he*?"

"Dana Thomas," both B.J. and Dana said at once.

"What's he doing here?" Tom demanded of B.J., ignoring Dana's outstretched hand.

"I live here." It was Dana who answered and this time he got Tom Sutherland's full attention.

"Does Albert Zurow know about this...arrangement?" Tom Sutherland glared from B.J. to Dana and back.

But it was Dana who took the initiative in answering. "As a matter of fact, Zurow found the place for us."

At Tom's look of disbelief, B.J. hastily added, " Mister Zurow didn't know I was a woman, because we arrived before our resumes got here and—"

"I don't believe I caught your name?" Dana rocked on his toes as he studied Tom. "Or what this has to do with you?"

"I'm Tom Sutherland, IPPS office in Miami," he said curtly without turning his attention from B.J.

Dana absorbed this new information with interest. He had known IPPS was sending a trouble shooter, but he hadn't expected it to be his house-mate's ex-husband. So this was Tom Sutherland. What a jerk. No wonder B.J. hated men.

"IPPS can't condone this arrangement, Betty Jo." He shook his head disapprovingly. "There's no question now but that you'll have to leave the job."

"Tom, I warn you, I'll file discrimination charges," B.J. repeated. "This living arrangement is strictly business, and if ChemCorp has no problem with it, IPPS shouldn't."

"You want me to believe that you're living with this guy Thomas and it's strictly business?" Tom sneered. "No way, Betty Jo."

"Because you would play it for all it's worth?" B.J. lifted an eyebrow. "Don't judge every man by yourself, Tom."

"It's a setup too cozy for a real man not to take advantage of," he stated with certainty, "and if word gets around the company about what's going on, your career with IPPS will be over."

"Wait a minute, Sutherland," Dana took a menacing step toward the other man, and B.J. noticed that he was half a head taller than her ex-husband. "The lady told you how it is, and I suggest you take her word for it. It's a business arrangement like she said, necessitated by a shortage of living quarters. If you don't buy it, I just may have to file a complaint of my own." His hands automatically became fists, and he flexed his arms. "Or something."

Tom took a step backward. "Okay, okay. We'll leave it at that—for the moment." He looked at B.J. "I won't mention this in my report, as a favor to you, but if anything else happens on this job, I'm not responsible for what IPPS does next. As it is, I'm going to have a tough time convincing them to leave you here with Albert Zurow making noise about contract clauses."

"Thank you, Tom," B.J. said sincerely. I'll see that you don't regret this."

"Can I show you out?" Dana asked with icy politeness, "If the consultation is over?"

Without another word to B.J., Tom followed Dana to the door.

"Nice meeting you, Thomas," he said automatically, then paused in the doorway. "Strange we haven't met before."

"Just our good fortune, I guess," Dana said wryly.

Ignoring the insult, Tom asked, "Been with the company long?"

"About fifteen years; got in on the ground floor." He opened the door and waited for Tom to walk through. "Have a good trip back. Tell Benny I'll call him about a golf game next time I'm in." Benjamin Whipple was president of IPPS and maintained his office at the Miami headquarters. Only his close friends called him Benny. Tom Sutherland looked suitably impressed.

The wind caught the door and it took all Dana's strength to keep it from slamming shut as he watched B.J.'s ex-husband make his way to the unfamiliar car he had noticed parked by the Escort when Yancy Webb dropped him off.

Webb had commented that maybe B.J. was entertaining a visitor and he would be sure to follow up on it, but explaining that was her problem. The tropical storm was imminent now, and he fervently hoped that Tom Sutherland got off the island before it hit. Another day of him in St. Croix would be a day too many.

B.J. was sitting on the sofa. A more forlorn and dejected figure would be hard to imagine.

His first impulse was to walk over there, pull her into his arms, and tell her everything was going to be fine. But he was neither a liar, nor a fool and that kind of statement would require him to be one or the other.

"Pardon me for saying it again, but it's not the end of the world." He took the chair closest to the sofa.

"It might as well be." She shook her head. "Why did they have to send him? Last I heard he was still on the West Coast."

"You got lucky?" Dana tried to lighten her mood but his glib answer failed its mission.

"There's nothing he'd like better than see me fired, and if I stay I probably will be, which would just prove his opinion of me had been right all along." She took a shuddering breath. "I should have agreed to leave now."

"Come on, B.J., get a handle on this. You've never struck me as a quitter...or a dummy." He grinned at her. "So why would you want to walk away without a fight?"

"Because I know Tom Sutherland. He was furious when I went to work for IPPS, said I'd just done it to spite him, and that I'd never make it through the program."

"Did you?" Dana asked quietly.

"Did I what?" she asked in confusion.

"Do it to spite him?"

"No," she said quickly, then after a thoughtful moment added, "Well, maybe it was partly that. I had married Tom right out of high school and worked to put him through the training program. I typed a lot of his material. I looked at the prints and discussed them with him. I even helped him with the questions when he studied for tests."

"So the job was familiar to you?" he asked.

"Yes, and I found it interesting. When Tom left me and I had to think about working again after all those years of staying home, wherever home was at the moment, I decided to enter the program myself." She paused, then went on. "I was hired without any help from Tom. I studied hard and made operator. Now here I am."

When she finished speaking the only sound in the room was the shutters rattling in the wind. Then Dana broke the silence.

"You haven't told me why he left you." For a moment, he thought she was going to refuse to tell him and he wondered if he had been wrong to ask.

"There was another woman, of course. It was after he got promoted to management in the West Coast office. Faye worked there." She sighed. "It's a predictable story. The pretty young secretary, the boring stay-at-home wife."

"He was a fool," Dana said flatly. What man would leave B.J. for any woman?

"No, I was the fool," she said miserably. "I didn't even suspect anything for a couple of years. I—"

A sudden gust of wind was accompanied by a loud crack as the trunk of a nearby palm tree broke and the top fell against the glass veranda. At that moment the lights went out.

B.J. stopped in mid-sentence. "We should see about some candles."

"Not yet," he said quietly as he reached across the darkness to take her hand, then prompted, "He broke your trusting heart?" He wanted to strangle the man with his bare hands for hurting her. Was it any wonder she had no trust left to give?

"I wanted a baby," she went on, talking almost to herself now. "Tom said we didn't need children until we could settle down, so I waited. Then we bought the house in Anaheim, and I thought the time had come, but still he said we should wait a little longer. Then," she gave a brittle laugh that was almost a sob, "he told me that he wanted a divorce, that he was going to marry Faye."

Dana gripped her hand, knowing she wasn't finished but wishing she didn't have to go through the pain she suffered in the telling.

"I begged him to wait, to go with me for counseling, but he said no. He had to have the divorce now, because Faye was pregnant with his child."

Dana swore softly and moved to the sofa to take B.J. in his arms and hold her while she cried as if her heart was breaking, the sound muffled by the keening wind. He cradled her head against his shoulder and stroked her hair, giving silent comfort until she quieted. Then he lifted her chin and kissed each swollen eyelid, tasting the salty wetness on her long lashes. His mouth moved gently to her forehead, her cheeks, the curve of her slender neck just below her ear, before his lips claimed hers in a slow deliberate communion of sympathy that needed no words.

Ever so slowly, he pulled away and stood. He took her hand and brought her to stand facing him and said huskily, "I want you. Will you let me show you how much?"

"I—we can't do this. It would make what Tom suspected true."

Dana wrapped his arms around her and drew her close. "We have the name. We may as well have the game." His lips touched hers with gentle persuasion.

She shivered and pressed against him.

He deepened the kiss, and they were oblivious to the worsening storm around them.

Taking her hand, he led her toward his bedroom, then stopped to embrace her again. He cupped her face and slanted his mouth over hers in a long kiss, his hands moving possessively over her back.

Taking her shoulders gently, he gazed into her glazed eyes. "I love you, Betty Jo Sutherland. Never doubt that for one moment."

He led her to his bed and removed her shorts and tee shirt. Even in his state of arousal, he noticed that she wore scant yellow underthings that matched the color of her striped shirt. He made quick work of shedding his own clothes and pulled her to him in a close embrace that left no doubt of his desire. With slow deliberation, he lowered her to the cool sheets and covered her shivering body with kisses until she was warm and wanting. He caressed her firm body, memorizing every hill and valley with his gentle touch. And when her body told him that she wanted more, he entered her and their bodies blazed with a need too long unfulfilled. When their passion reached its zenith and was finally spent, they lay sated in each other's arms and slept.

The clock had stopped when the palm tree fell and the room was still in darkness as Dana lay awake. He listened to the sound of wind-driven rain pelting against the windows and knew the storm had not yet spent its fury. Nature's violent show of force echoed his inner turmoil. He dozed fitfully and woke with Betty Jo lying in his arms and pondered his dilemma. It was true, what he'd told her. He loved her. Would she accept the love he offered or reject it? Finally an exhausted sleep overtook his turbulent thoughts.

CHAPTER ELEVEN

B.J. awoke in the darkness and felt a moment of panic when she remembered last night and the man who had said he loved her. She had been Tom Sutherland's wife for ten years and had thought she loved him, but until now she had never really understood the meaning of the word. It was the special feeling between a woman and a man that she had experienced with Dana Thomas. For the first time she had received in full measure what she had given. Her ex-husband had been unwilling or unable to give of himself completely, but she had not understood that before.

But what did that matter now? The job would soon be over, and it was unlikely she and Dana would be sent to the same location. She wasn't willing to go back to being the live-in maid she had been for Tom, following wherever he went with no life of her own. She sighed again. It seemed that love always came with a high price tag for her, one she was no longer willing to pay.

Careful not to make a sound, B.J. eased from Dana's bed and gathered her clothing. She tip-toed out of his room into the dark hallway. The power was still off, so she showered in lukewarm water, leaving enough for her house-mate. Then she dressed and went out onto the veranda. The tropical storm had wreaked its havoc and swept back out to sea, leaving a swath of debris in its path. The eerie quiet preceding the storm had been replaced by a cacophony of cheerful birdsong.

What was she going to do? Perhaps it would be best if she left, especially now after what had happened last night, but she had vowed to prove Tom Sutherland wrong and leaving would be admitting defeat. Yet if she stayed on there was the threat of getting fired and the even more frightening threat of Dana Thomas. She seemed damned either way.

When Dana awoke again it was late morning and the storm was over. His first thought was of B.J. and how vulnerable she was underneath her tough facade, and he was filled with a fierce need to protect her from now on. He reminded himself that B.J. Sutherland was a woman who had made it in a man's world and being equal was important to her. His relationship with her would have to be different from what he once had with Kate. They would have to find their way together in uncharted territory, both involved in careers that might conflict at times, but he was more than willing to make the effort for the woman he loved. They could make it work.

His eyes felt gritty from too much sleep, and his body was damp from the oppressive heat. A shower was what he needed now, then he'd find his love and they would talk.

Showered and dressed, Dana found B.J. on the veranda. She was facing the Caribbean and appeared to be lost in thought. He stopped a moment to admire the curve of her body and the way her head tilted with such enticing charm before he made her aware of his presence.

"Deep thoughts, my love?" Dana said in a low voice.

She turned quickly, meeting his eyes, then glanced away. "We have to talk."

"Yes, we do." He crossed the space between them and reached out to take her hand, but she evaded his touch.

"Last night was a mistake." Her voice was ragged, as if she had been running a long way. "It should never have happened."

"I took advantage of you in a weak moment, and now you're sorry?" he asked quietly.

"No, I was as much to blame as you," she admitted, "more than you."

"Just for the record, I want you to know that I meant

what I told you last night."

"And also for the record, I want you to know there was never anyone but Tom in my life. Until now."

"I'm glad."

"After my marriage ended, I had an urge to go out with someone, anyone, to prove that I was a desirable woman," she confessed, "but I couldn't bear the thought of another rejection, so I never did. Then I found a better way of proving my worth."

"Your job?"

"Yes, it was much more certain than depending on a man for validation."

"I think we both used our work as our salvation from grief," Dana agreed, "but that's over now, B.J. We have a future...together."

"No." She thought of Tom's admonitions. "I have to keep my mind on the plant. I can't let anything else happen, anything at all."

"You mean that, don't you?" His voice echoed his hurt and bewilderment.

"It's nothing personal," she assured him. "It's just that..."

"*Nothing personal?*" He made an effort to control his mounting anger. "Then your definition of personal is not the same as mine."

"I mean," She took a deep breath and tried to explain. "It is nothing you've done. We just wouldn't be able to make this work. I hope we can go back to the way things were...or I really will have to take a transfer."

She left him no choice. If she went, it would all be over. If she stayed, there might still be a chance he could change her mind.

"Okay." He shrugged as if his world had not just collapsed on top of him. "You will decide what our relationship will be, but I'm here if you change your mind."

"I won't, Dana." She looked sad but determined, and he knew convincing her otherwise would be the most impossible thing he had ever tried to do.

The roads on the island were almost impassable with the refuse left from the night's storm. Dana drove but only because it was his turn. They had agreed on the Cormorant as it was fairly close, and they'd not yet had morning coffee due to the villa being without electricity.

B.J. sat as far toward the passenger door as she could, fearing an accidental brush with Dana's hand as he shifted gears. If he touched her, she might turn to a blob of jelly right before his eyes. Too much had happened, too fast, and she hadn't gotten her emotions back under control yet, but she would. All she had to do was keep her goal in mind and the rest would be easy. Wouldn't it? So why did the profile of the man who had declared his love last night make her want to forget goals, forget her vows never to place her faith and fate in the hands of any man again?

Maybe Dana Thomas was different. Maybe he would know how to cherish and protect her while still giving her the freedom to be herself. No, she couldn't have it both ways. If she wanted equal rights on the playing field, then she couldn't also sit in a box seat. She'd had that, and it had made her a prisoner. Seeing Tom again last night had reminded her of what her marriage had been like. Even now he tried to control her. It must have been the repercussions of her encounter with Tom that had sent her headlong into the arms of Dana Thomas. She stole a sidelong glance at him, silent and unsmiling behind the wheel, gaze never leaving the road, and sighed softly. Why did he have to be so heart-stopping handsome? Why did every pore in her body yearn for him?

The Cormorant Beach Club was almost deserted as most of the islanders were still recovering from the storm damage. Dana and B.J. ordered a pot of coffee first thing. They sat on the rain-washed terrace, savoring the strong brew, and made stilted conversation.

"Do you think there may have been any damage at the plant?" B.J. asked.

"I doubt it," Dana shrugged. "These places are used to tropical storms and hurricanes. They're built to withstand the forces of nature."

"Just the same, I'm glad it didn't blow in on my shift," B.J. said. "At lease, nobody can blame me for that."

The arrival of their food was a welcome diversion. When they had finished their omelets, they lingered over third cups of coffee, both reluctant to return to the intimacy of the villa with half a day stretching ahead of them.

Finally, Dana spoke. "Do you have any plans to use the car this afternoon?"

B.J. shook her head. "I have laundry to do. Unless you planned to get some sleep and the noise—"

"No, I thought I'd play a round of golf, if the course is open at the Buccaneer."

He was going to play golf, and he hadn't ask her to go along. B.J. remembered the day they had played together and the evening that followed. She wondered if he would ask one of the other operators this time. Frank Kelly would be off until tomorrow, same as her, but he could have asked her just the same, unless he didn't want to risk getting beat again!

B.J. stood. "Then we'd better get moving." She laid a bill on the waiter's tray, large enough to cover gratuity, and picked up her backpack. This was the way it was going to be, so she might as well get used to it. No easy camaraderie like they had before. They had crossed the line, and there was no going back. Why was it impossible for a man and woman to be just friends without the involvement of hormones? If she was honest, she would admit that going beyond friendship had always been one-sided until Dana, and she wanted something more than friendship now just as much as he did. But she was not willing to pay the price.

The humidity seemed higher than B.J. could ever re-member as she climbed into the car with Frank Kelly the fol-lowing morning. Perhaps it was the aftermath of the tropical storm. In any case, she hadn't slept well even knowing that Dana Thomas was at work and his bed empty. Images of the night before kept her awake for hours and then vivid dreams had disturbed her sleep. She had to get a handle on things and work was a welcome diversion.

After a shot by shot account of yesterday's golf game with Dana, concluding with how he'd birdied the last hole to win by three strokes, Frank fell silent.

Dana hadn't been in top form yesterday, she thought

with perverse satisfaction. She knew he was a better golfer than Frank Kelly and could imagine how it irked him to lose and have Frank brag about it to everyone.

"I heard your ex-husband was here Monday." Frank turned to look at B.J. as he spoke, but she kept her eyes on the busy highway when she answered.

"You heard right."

"I don't guess you saw him, since you were working midnights?" He glanced back at the road and swerved just in time to avoid a car which had slowed before turning left.

"I saw him."

"Did he get off the island before the storm?" Frank continued doggedly.

"Far as I know."

"So that's how you made it in the training program," he went on. "A little help from hubby or was he ex-hubby already when you went through?"

Now he was getting to the crux of his cross-examination. She ignored the first remark and clarified the relationship. "Ex."

"So he gave you an operator's license instead of alimony? Smart thinking on his part." He swiveled his head to give her a meaningful grin.

"Look, Kelly, none of this is any of your business, but since you've made it so, let me assure you that Tom Sutherland had nothing to do with my acceptance into the program nor my passing the operator's exams." B.J. clenched her fists in her lap to keep from taking a swing at his smug face.

"Word's out he plans to fire you. Any truth in that?"

"Oh?" B.J. made an effort to control her anger. "For what reason?"

Frank hesitated as if trying to remember. "I think it was incompetence, or maybe it was immorality?"

B.J. took a deep breath. "Nobody can fire me without just cause, Kelly, and I'm not guilty on either count."

Frank turned into the parking lot of ChemCorp and eased the car to a stop but left the air-conditioner running. "You may not be guilty of anything, honey, but it has caused some talk, you and Thomas sharing the villa I mean. That, plus all the problems with equipment on your shift." He shrugged. "Albert Zurow is not a happy man."

"Then Zurow needs to tell me, not you, Kelly," she said,

then added, "Unless you've been designated his spokesman?"

"I'm only trying to help you," Frank said smoothly, "and I've got an idea that might give a different slant to the situation."

"Such as?" She raised one eyebrow.

"Well, I thought if you and I go out together, sort of make it a point to be seen..." He laughed and placed a hand on her knee. "Maybe we dance cheek to cheek? Then I'd let the word get around that we had something going..."

B.J. pushed his hand away and jerked open the car door. She slid to the ground and turned to glare at him. "I don't like your idea worth a hoot, Kelly. I'll take my chances on getting fired any day before I'd be seen any place but work with you."

She slammed the door with more force than necessary and walked toward the building while a surprised Frank Kelly looked after her.

"Bitch," he mumbled as he turned off the ignition and followed. "Ungrateful bitch."

B.J. felt as if she was on a tightrope in midair without a net below her. She had to watch her step every minute at the plant to make sure things went well, because she knew that Albert Zurow was keeping a constant eye on her. Then she had to do likewise at the villa to avoid any personal contact with her house-mate, although so far they had met only in passing. She could feel his eyes on her, too, and the worst of it was that she didn't have a clue what he was thinking.

Dana had taken his cue from her and maintained a polite, aloof distance, but sometimes she caught him looking at her with a wistful expression that made her want to throw herself into his arms and say, "I'm yours."

She had finished a week of day shifts and was working midnights again with only one shift remaining. The feed pump had arrived and been put in service, so they would be back to full load soon. Maybe then Albert Zurow would be in a better mood.

The blast of cool air from the control room was a welcome respite from the sweltering heat as B.J. opened the
door and stepped inside.

Dana was engrossed with the indicators on the bench
board and did not notice her approach as she stood looking
at his broad hunched shoulders with longing. As if sensing
her need, he suddenly turned and met her eyes.

"Everything..." She stopped and took an uneven breath
before she could finish. "Is everything going okay?"

"So far, so good." He crossed two fingers on his right
hand. "We're raising the load on the boiler, and I think we've
got the fuel-air ratio about right. Will you be okay with finishing this?"

Dana's patronizing tone brought B.J.'s fantasy world back
to reality in a hurry. "I think I can handle it, Thomas," she
told him frostily, "and if not, I can always turn it over to
Kelly."

B.J. looked toward the other operator's chair and saw
that it was still occupied by Pete Marshall. Frank surely didn't
need a nap already. He must be getting coffee.

"Just keep a close eye on it," Dana warned and turned
toward Pete. "I'll be in the parking lot when you're ready,
Marshall."

He made a hasty exit through the door, almost bumping
into Frank Kelly who came rushing in.

Pete swiveled his chair around, and Frank gave him a
thumbs up sign as they exchanged places. Then only B.J.,
Frank, and their two trainees remained in the control room.
B.J. continued to increase the firing rate on the boiler, being
careful to keep the fuel and air flow balanced. The ratio
looked good according to the indicators, but she was uneasy.
Perhaps it was because she could feel Frank watching her.
Could Dana have asked him to? Didn't anyone give her credit
for being able to bring a boiler back up to full load? Well, she
would show them.

"Lohr," she turned to speak to her trainee who was returning from the kitchen with two cups of coffee, "I'd like you
to go out to the boiler area and have a look at things."

"Sure, Miss Sutherland." He gave B.J. a cup, put the
other on the desk, and went to do her bidding.

A few minutes passed as B.J. sipped her hot coffee. Then
she glanced back at the board and saw that the boiler was

losing pressure. She quickly pushed a button to increase the flow of fuel, and seconds later a sound like a bomb exploding reverberated through the control room.

B.J. looked toward Frank, her eyes filled with horror. "Oh, my God," she breathed softly.

"The boiler," they both mouthed in unison.

CHAPTER TWELVE

For a moment B.J. was too stunned to move, then she went into action. "Desmond, take my place here," she ordered and tore out of the control room at a run.

The plant was filled with smoke and coal dust. B.J. pulled a handkerchief from her pocket and tied it around her nose and mouth as she ran. The stench of flue gas sickened her, and the roar of steam escaping from the boiler was almost deafening. Groping her way through the haze, she stumbled upon the inert body of Lohr a few feet away.

The trainee must have instinctively turned and tried to run to safety but the blast had caught him in the back for he lay face down on the concrete floor, his clothes soaked with scalding water. She dared not turn him over for fear of doing further harm to his burned body, but she knew that she might not have sufficient strength to lift his face off the floor and drag him to safety. A fine mist of hot steam still sprayed from the ruptured tubes, and B.J. became aware of the danger for both of them remaining so close to the boiler. She dropped to her knees and placed her hands under Lohr's armpits and tugged at his limp body.

The heavy man did not budge.

"Dear God," she moaned softly, "please help me." She took a deep breath of air and coughed. Tears stung her eyes, and her skin tingled painfully where the steam made contact. She tugged harder and this time Lohr's prone body responded.

In the dimly lit parking lot, Dana drummed on the Escort's steering wheel as he waited impatiently for Pete Marshall. He wished he had been able to bring up the boiler before his shift ended for he felt uneasy about leaving an inexperienced operator like B.J. to do it alone. From what he had seen of Frank Kelly's operating expertise, he wouldn't be any help in an emergency. Sometimes he wondered how guys like Kelly had ever passed their operator's exams in the first place or why IPPS employed them. He knew for certain if Benny Whipple was aware of Frank Kelly's job performance, he'd fire him in a heartbeat.

And what was keeping Pete? Why couldn't Frank relieve him on time so they could get out of here?

Finally, he saw a figure walking slowly toward the car and started the engine, turning the air conditioner on high.

"Sorry," Pete said as he got into the car and put his lunch box on the floorboard. He wiped his brow. "Damn, it's hot."

Dana nodded without answering and put the Ford into reverse and backed out of the parking space. Just as he changed gears, preparing to head for the gate, the sound of an explosion rent the air. The two men looked at each other in alarm.

Dana swore softly and swerved back into a parking space. He left the car at a run with Pete Marshall close behind.

He tore through the door and headed for the boiler area. In the smoke-filled plant, he had trouble breathing for a moment and grabbed a handkerchief to cover his face. He could make out two figures in the gloom, one being dragged. His gut twisted with fear. What if B.J. was hurt? He leaped toward them and pushed aside the one who was dragging the other.

"Here, let me." He carefully hooked his hands under the unconscious body, realizing with relief that it was not B.J.

Pete was right behind them. "What happened? Who's hurt?"

"Lohr's burned," B.J. shouted above the noise of the steam. She coughed, then went on. "He was checking the boiler when it blew."

"Call an ambulance," Dana barked. "Tell them to hurry."

He eased Lohr into the control room and let him down gently.

"What happened? Who—" Frank began as he got up from the control panel.

"Get on the other phone and call Hess Oil and ask for their emergency crew to get over here right away," Dana told him. "Then call Zurow."

Desmond left the controls and hovered just behind B.J. "Is he hurt bad?" he asked fearfully.

"He's probably got third degree burns," Dana told him in a low voice. "And he's in shock. Get a blanket from supplies if you can find one. We need to keep him warm."

Dana stepped to the control board and took a quick check while Pete and Frank made calls. Then he looked at B.J. who hovered over Lohr, her skin turning a bright pink.

"You're burned, too," he said as he crossed the room to stand beside her. "You need ice on your skin."

She made no move to follow his suggestion but continued with her ineffective ministrations to the unconscious trainee.

Dana reached out and took her hand, pulling her toward the kitchen.

"No, I have to take care of—" she protested.

"Right now," he said firmly.

In the tiny kitchen, he jerked open the refrigerator and took out an ice tray. He dumped it in the sink then grabbed two cubes. He began gently rubbing them along B.J.'s face.

"But Lohr—" she began again.

"Everything is under control," he told her. He handed B.J. an ice cube, but she waved it away.

"I can wait until—"

"Take this and use it on your arms." He looked at her shirt and realized it was plastered to her body. "No, wait," he added, "First you need to take off your top."

"No, I can't—" she began, so he put down the ice and unbuttoned her shirt, carefully peeled it off her shivering body.

She was wearing a pale yellow satin bra, and it was soaked, too. He unhooked its front fastener and removed it, averting his eyes from her with effort. Then he gave her the ice again and commanded with a rough edge to his voice,

"Now rub...all over."

"I called Zurow, and he's—" Frank Kelly stuck his head around the door and stopped in mid-sentence. "Holy—"

"Stop gawking, Kelly, and get back to the control board before we have another disaster on our hands," Dana said sharply as B.J. covered her bare bosom with her arms. "Call Webb and Evans, get them out here. We need all the help we can get."

From the noise in the control room, it was obvious that the crew from Hess Oil had arrived.

"I have to—" B.J. made a move to reach for her shirt, but Dana stopped her.

"They don't need you, B.J. I told you everything is under control." He placed another ice cube into her hand. "You must take care of yourself now, or you'll have a very painful burn."

"I—I guess this is the end for me," B.J. coughed on a sob in her throat.

"Can you tell me what happened?" Dana asked.

B.J. nodded. "Everything was going fine. The indicators showed a good fuel-air balance, but I asked Lohr to go out and check just to be sure." She took a ragged breath and coughed again. "Then the gauge showed we were losing pressure, so I increased the air flow."

Dana shook his head and groaned. "You should have decreased the fuel. It would have been less likely to explode that way."

Tears formed in her eyes and rolled down her cheeks. "Then I—I'm responsible for a man being badly hurt. I deserve to be fired."

"I didn't say that," Dana amended quickly. "It was a judgment call, and it was just bad luck that a trainee was at the site when the explosion happened."

They heard the sound of a siren in the distance and then Albert Zurow appeared in the doorway with Frank Kelly right behind him.

"Now I want to know—" At the sight of B.J.'s bare back he stopped and sucked in his breath, "Miss Sutherland, what is the meaning of this?"

"I can explain, Mister—" she began.

"Get dressed and report to my office im—"

"She's burned, Zurow," Dana interrupted in a firm voice,

"and she'd not reporting anywhere until she's had first aid and rest. I'm taking her home."

Albert Zurow's outraged eyes met Dana's unflinching gaze.

After a long silence, he nodded curtly. "All right, Thomas." Then to B.J. he added, "I'll expect a full report from you on this...entire incident at your earliest convenience."

He left then, slamming the door behind him. Dana looked at B.J. and smiled grimly. "Let's put your shirt on and get out of here."

B.J. numbly acquiesced while her mind tried to sort out what had happened in the last hour. She had made an error in judgment which had resulted in a horrible accident to Lohr. Dana had incurred Zurow's wrath by taking her part. Maybe she wasn't capable of being a power plant operator. Maybe Tom had been right after all.

After a shower and change of clothes, Dana checked to see that B.J. was comfortable and then returned to the plant. He had obtained a soothing antiseptic balm from the Hess Oil emergency crew and seen to B.J.'s burns. Then he'd fixed her a rum and fruit juice drink while she showered off the fly ash in lukewarm water, and afterwards put her to bed, all over her adamant protests that she didn't need his help. From what he surmised by Albert Zurow's reaction, she was going to need all the help she could get. And even then, it might not be enough.

There were more cars in the parking lot when he arrived back at the plant. He assumed that Webb and Evans and perhaps some of the day crew had reported in. Going into the control room, he saw Frank Kelly still at the board and Carl Evans occupied B.J.'s chair. Two new trainees were assisting, making him wonder if Desmond had accompanied Lohr to the hospital.

Carl looked up as Dana walked in and asked quickly, "Is Miss Sutherland okay?"

"She's got first degree burns from trying to get Lohr to safety," Dana answered grimly. He still felt Kelly, being the more experienced operator, should have been on top of things and not allowed B.J. to go into the boiler area to bring out Lohr after the explosion.

As if sensing Dana's unspoken thoughts, Frank offered an excuse. "Sutherland tore out of here when the big bang came before I could tell her to stay put and let me do it. Both of us couldn't leave the controls at a crucial time like that." He shook his head. "It's really too bad she didn't ask my advice before she increased the air flow. That decision could have cost Lohr his life."

"What's done is done," Dana said curtly. "Monday morning quarterbacking won't change it."

"Right," Frank agreed heartily. "This time I think she blew it in more ways than one." He chuckled at his own pun but none of the others joined in. "Albert Zurow has had enough of her blunders."

Ignoring his remark, Dana asked of Evans, "Anyone in the boiler area now?"

"Yeah, Webb is supervising the clean-up and I think Pete went on back to the villa."

"I'll see if they need any more help," Dana said and left the control room before Frank Kelly said something he couldn't overlook. Not only was the guy incompetent, he seemed to have a personal vendetta against B.J. that was totally unjustified. She'd done nothing to earn his dislike except refuse to go out with him, but maybe in Kelly's eyes that was grounds for revenge.

Wait a minute. A thought smacked him with as much force as the heat and acrid smell of the ruptured boiler tube. Frank Kelly worked the same shift as B.J. He had been on duty every time something had gone wrong. Could he be responsible for what was happening? And if so, how could it be proved?

"Thomas." He came back abruptly to the present at the sound of Zurow's voice. "Is Miss Sutherland all right?"

Dana repeated his earlier report in the control room and when he had finished, Zurow shook his head.

"I should have known a woman in the work place would be big trouble but her credentials were excellent. However, I plan to call the IPPS office in the morning and ask for a replacement."

"Mister Zurow, would you consider giving her one more

chance? She did rush in to rescue her trainee without any thought for her own safety. That ought to be worth something."

"I'm sorry, Thomas." Albert Zurow regarded him intently. "I must say after finding the two of you in a compromising position for the second time I wonder exactly what your relation to Miss Sutherland may be." When Dana started to protest, the supervisor raised his hand and continued. "That is irrelevant now. Rumor has it the union is going to order the local employees to walk out if she stays, so that settles it."

Dana clamped his mouth closed and counted to ten. Then he asked without expression. "Do you need me here for cleanup?"

"No, I believe Webb can handle things until the day shift gets in. Marshall will be back then."

"Then I think I'll stop by the hospital and check on Lohr and then get some sleep."

Zurow looked at his watch. "Midnight. I may go home for a while myself, though I doubt that I'll be able to sleep after all this."

Dana found the St. Croix Hospital parking lot almost deserted and wondered if he should have waited until morning to stop, but as long as he was here, it wouldn't hurt to at least check on Lohr's condition.

The hospital was small by mainland standards and after Dana convinced the nurse on duty to allow him access to Lohr, he had no difficulty locating him. He was in a section which might be defined as intensive care with beds in private cubicles monitored by a central nurse's station. A tangle of wires and tubes connected the trainee to various machines and bottles, and he was lying on his stomach with his back swathed in bandages.

Dana stepped to the side of the bed and peered at Lohr's face which was half hidden by a pillow.

His eyes were open, and he said a groggy hello.

"Hurting much?" Dana asked with concern.

"Not too bad," Lohr answered. "Is Miss Sutherland—"

"She's fine," Dana assured him. "Just concerned about you."

"That's one brave lady. She dragged me out of there." He gave Dana a weak smile. "I wish to thank her."

"I'll pass it on."

"Tell her that I saw something she should know. The calibration on the fuel flow?"

Dana pulled up a chair and sat close to the bed. "Yeah, Lohr, go on, what about it?"

"It didn't match what was showing on the control board. I don't see how—"

"Are you sure about this?" Maybe it was the pain shots they had given him. Maybe he wasn't thinking straight.

"I'm sure. I double-checked and wrote it down. That was when..." He closed his eyes and grimaced as if remembering what happened next was painful.

"Where did you put your notes, Lohr?"

"In my shirt pocket."

"And they cut your clothes off?" Dana asked almost to himself.

"I don't know. I don't remember anything after that till the ambulance came."

"Don't worry about it," Dana stood. "I'll check into it. You'll swear to what you've told me?"

"Yes, but I don't want to cause any trouble." The trainee looked fearful.

"There is trouble already," Dana told him. "If we can't prove this explosion wasn't B.J., uh, Miss Sutherland's fault, she will lose her job."

"Then find my notes, Mister Thomas. She's a nice lady."

Dana lost no time in seeking the head nurse on duty and explaining the importance of locating Lohr's discarded clothing. It took all of his skills of persuasion to convince her that he should be allowed access to them and then almost an hour to trace them down, but when he left the hospital he was in possession of a small notebook which contained evidence that the calibration on the fuel flow indicator did not match the numbers on the control board from which B.J. was operating. If he wasn't mistaken, she had made her decision to increase air flow on incorrect information. As he drove back to the villa, he retraced the events leading up to the shift change. Frank Kelly had been late. Where had he been? What had he been doing? Even if Kelly was guilty of anything as devious as deliberately changing the settings, how could he ever prove it?

The lights were on in the villa when he parked the car. Dana hurried to unlock the gate and check on B.J. He found her sitting on the sofa, her head in her hands and quickly crossed the distance between them. "What is it?" he asked with concern. "What's wrong?"

"This," she pointed to a small voodoo doll lying beside her. It had hair of yellow yarn and pins sticking all over its crudely made body.

He picked it up for a closer look. "Where did you get this?" he demanded.

"Something woke me. A sound at the door, I think. I thought it might be you, so I got up and went to see. I didn't hear anyone, so I opened the door and this," she indicated the doll with a shudder, "was there."

"Nobody has a key to the gate except us. They, whoever did this, must have thrown it over the fence." He frowned. "They must have known you were here alone and meant to frighten you."

"Well, they succeeded." She began to cry again.

He enfolder her in his arms and held her close while she wept.

"They don't need to scare me off the island. I'll go willingly now."

"Hold on a minute." Dana held her away from him so he could look into her eyes. "I've stumbled onto some information that may prove you were set up for what happened."

"Set up?" She looked dubious.

"Right. I just talked with Lohr, and he told me the calibration on the air flow didn't jive with the control panel readings."

"What would that have to do..." she began doubtfully.

"It would mean someone deliberately changed the settings so you would carry a fuel ratio that was too rich and the over-fueling would cause an explosion. Now the question is who?"

"Surely no one would..." She stopped and looked at him sadly. "I can't believe that of anyone, not to endanger another person's life."

"There wasn't supposed to be anyone out there. I think whoever did this just planned to damage the equipment and make you look incompetent."

"They did this to get me - fired?"

"Well, word was out that you had one more mistake and that was all." He took a handkerchief and gently wiped her bright cheeks. "Now try to remember what happened before the accident. Beginning with when you got to work."

"Well...Frank was late." B.J. frowned. "And when he relieved Pete, he gave him a thumbs up sign."

"Did this seem peculiar?"

"Not really, although I hadn't seen him do it before. Then he kept watching me, but I thought maybe you'd asked him to keep an eye on things while I was bringing up the boiler."

"You're every bit as good or better at operating than he is, B.J. so why would I do that?"

She gave him such a grateful smile that he couldn't resist the urge to kiss her. He brushed her lips lightly, and her spontaneous response was so receptive that his mouth lingered on hers in silent communion.

"Let me take you back to bed," he whispered huskily when he finally ended the kiss.

"Please do," she said tiredly.

He knew the voodoo doll had frightened her more than she was willing to admit. He also felt certain it was somehow related to Lohr's accident and the intent to drive her from the island.

He led her to the bedroom and sat down beside her single bed, holding her hand until she slept, but sleep did not come for Dana as he tried to figure out how to fit the pieces of the puzzle together and exonerate the woman he loved.

CHAPTER THIRTEEN

Waking in the predawn darkness, Dana eased his body from the chair beside B.J.'s bed and slipped quietly out of her room. The accident at the plant, her own injuries, and the voodoo encounter had left her so exhausted that she was still sleeping soundly. Dressing hurriedly, he quietly left the villa and stopped for Pete Marshall. The two of them grabbed a quick breakfast at a fast food place en route to work.

Frank Kelly met them at the front door of the plant.

"What's up, Frank?" Pete asked. "Someone else relieve your shift?"

Frank shook his head. "Nope, Zurow had us shut down, said it was the only way to avoid a walkout until the matter of B.J. Sutherland is settled."

"I'm guessing the boiler repair will be the official excuse?" Pete surmised aloud.

"Right." Frank grinned. "It looks like we've got a holiday for now. How about if we do a little celebrating?"

Pete returned Frank's grin. "What have you got in mind?"

"Well, for starters I need a little shut-eye. Then maybe nine holes of golf? After that we could have dinner at the Calabash and party the night away."

"Sounds good to me, man," Pete agreed, then turned to Dana. "What about you, Thomas?"

Dana opened his mouth to refuse, then had second thoughts. "Count me in for the Calabash. What time?"

"Sundown," Frank told him. "We just might feel like playing eighteen today."

"I'll be there," Dana answered, then turned to Pete. "Could you ride back to the villa with Frank? I need to check on something here."

"Sure," Pete agreed. "I may even catch a few more winks myself.

"Let's see if Yancy and Evans want to make it a foursome today," Frank said as the two men headed toward the parking lot.

Dana stood watching them until they drove away. It was hard to believe anyone would stoop so low as to endanger human lives in order to put an innocent woman down, but he was certain now that one or both of them had done so. Of the two, Frank Kelly had the most obvious reason. B.J. had stood her ground with him from the beginning. The more he had badgered her, the more she'd dug in her heels.

If Dana could only come up with solid proof of his suspicions she might not lose her fight to prove her competence. If he failed, her days at ChemCorp, and probably at IPPS, were numbered.

He went into the control room where the trainees were tidying up and preparing to leave. Desmond was still sitting at the board, head in hands, and he looked up morosely as Dana walked by.

"Mister Thomas?" he said softly.

Dana stopped. "Yes?"

"How is Miss Sutherland?"

"She'll be okay. Right now she's still exhausted and in shock."

"I think—" He looked around to see if anyone else was in earshot and finding no one, he continued, "I think there's something you ought to know."

Dana pulled up a nearby chair and sat down beside the trainee. "Okay, shoot."

"That work order Miss Sutherland said she wrote? About the ID fan?"

"Yes, go on," Dana urged quietly.

"I saw it."

"You saw it?" Dana repeated. "Where?"

"In her log book, like she said. Before the shift ended."

"Do you know what happened to it?" Dana asked when the trainee hesitated.

"I think it got thrown away while we were changing

shifts."

"By Lohr?" Dana prompted.

"No, sir. Mister Kelly was looking at her log. He took it out and threw it away."

"I see."

Desmond took a deep breath and resolutely went on. "That night Mister Marshall got sick?"

"Yes?" Dana resisted the urge to shake the trainee and demand that he get on with it.

"Mister Kelly came back to get him, and I saw him at the pump. When I spoke to him, he told me to get back to the control room and not to mention that he was out there. He said he was checking up on Miss Sutherland at Mister Zurow's orders, and she'd be mad if she knew."

"Have you told anyone about this?" Dana demanded.

"No, sir." Desmond shook his head. "He said he was doing it for Mister Zurow. I didn't have any reason to find it suspicious at the time."

"You don't believe that now?"

"I don't know what to believe, Mister Thomas. But Lohr is hurt bad The men are blaming Miss Sutherland, and I thought you ought to know what I saw."

"You did the right thing to tell me, Desmond. Would you be willing to swear to this in Albert Zurow's presence?"

"I don't want to get anyone in trouble." The trainee looked apprehensive. "Who would believe me anyway?"

"I believe you," Dana assured him. " I'll try to protect your confidence if I can, but a woman's job is on the line just because someone has an unjustified grudge against her. We have to stop her from being dismissed unfairly, don't we?"

Desmond mutely agreed, then added. "I just hope telling you doesn't get me dismissed, too."

"It won't," Dana promised grimly and sincerely hoped he was right. He had to get back to the villa and look in on B.J. Tonight he had some heavy partying to do, which meant he'd better grab some sleep so he would be alert.

The sun was just sinking below the blue-green waters of

the Caribbean as Dana wedged the Escort into a narrow space on Strand Street. He recognized another Ford parked in front of the Columbian Emeralds shop as he mounted the steps to the restaurant above it and knew the others had arrived before him. The West Indian dining spot was popular with tourists both for its food and entertainment. Dana elbowed his way through the crowd until he spotted the four men at a table with a view. Their animated faces and loud laughter told him they were feeling the effects of more than a day in the sun even before he joined them.

"Well, look who's here." Frank Kelly slapped the back of a vacant chair beside him and motioned for Dana. "We've just ordered another round of screw drivers, but you can probably catch our waitress and add one more."

"I'll wait for the next round," Dana told him as he sat down beside Frank. Fate must be smiling on him. This was exactly where he had hoped to be.

"Just left the villa, Thomas?" Carl Evans asked as he fixed slightly unfocused eyes on him. When Dana nodded, the man continued. "How is Miss Sutherland tonight?"

"Still pretty shaken up," Dana told him, "but otherwise alright."

"Doesh the li'le operator have her bags packed yet?" Pete Marshall asked in a slurred voice.

"No, should she?" Dana inquired coolly.

"Her eni-emi-aw, hell, fast deparshure is a done deal," Yancey told him in a smug voice.

"I hadn't heard," Dana answered drily as he picked up the menu and studied it intently.

The waitress came back then with drinks and took orders for dinner. Dana asked for chicken in peanut sauce as the inebriated four debated the merits of blackened dolphin versus shrimp and conch Calabash.

"Bring more screw drivers, sweet thing." Frank leered at the young waitress and patted her backside while Dana clenched his fists to keep from using them.

While they waited for their food, conversation turned to the day's golf game, and Dana was given a replay of every hole. The performance of the winning team of Kelly and Marshall grew ever more brilliant in the retelling, and Dana forced himself to look suitably impressed.

During dinner more drinks were ordered. Dana watched

Frank and gaged his state of sobriety. It was obvious he had a high tolerance to liquor from habitual drinking, and it would take more than normal consumption to loosen his tongue.

The restaurant grew more crowded. Loud talk and laughter competed with the vibrant beat of the steel drum music to raise the noise level to gigantic proportions. The room was hot and smoky. Dana unbuttoned his shirt collar and wiped the perspiration from his forehead. He reached for the frosty glass the waitress placed in front of him and just as he was about to quench his growing thirst, Frank stopped him.

"Wait. Les have a toast." Frank raised his own glass a bit unsteadily. "To the guys who won the battle of the sexshish."

"Hear, hear," Pete added with a lopsided grin.

"I didn't know there was one." Dana took a long drink and gave Frank a comradely look. "Tell me about it, ole buddy."

"Well," Frank lowered his voice, "we couldn't have a skirt invading our ter-tory, could we? So me and Pete took action."

"Affirm-tive action," Pete chimed in and chuckled. "I put the lizzard in 'er lunch box." He grinned proudly.

"You don't say?" Dana looked surprised. "And the other stuff? How did you two manage that?"

"Aw, it was easy," Frank boasted. "And Zurow never sush-suspected a thing."

"And 'er ex showin' up was a bonus we never counted on." Pete slapped the table top, and the four men laughed.

"Were you guys in on this, too?" Dana looked at Evans and Yancy.

"Nope, didn't have a clue," Carl Evans denied with obvious sincerity.

"Blowin' the boiler was Frank's idea," Pete admitted magnanimously.

"It could have killed someone." Dana caught Frank's arm in a hard grip and held his surprised gaze. "Did you think of that?"

Frank shrugged. "It was jush one of the islanders. No harm done."

"Why, you son-of-..." Dana stopped, forced himself to speak calmly. "You'll pay for this, Kelly. With your job, if I have anything to do with it."

"No way," Frank snarled, suddenly more sober. "You

can't prove anything. So you might as well kiss your li'le playmate goodbye. She's as good as gone."

"I've got plenty of proof," Dana warned. He looked at Evans and Yancy. "These guys can witness to your confession tonight."

Frank jerked his arm from Dana's grip and stood suddenly, overturning his chair. "I'm outta here. This plash stinks." He weaved toward the door with the others following.

Dana watched them pay their checks and depart, but he remained at the table, debating what to do. If he went to Zurow, he would have to depend on Yancy and Evans supporting his accusations or else involve the trainees.

"Another drink, sir?" The waitress smiled at him as she gathered up the empty glasses and placed them on a tray.

"No more," he told her. "Some coffee, please." The heat was stifling and he ought to get out of here, but he needed a little more time to decide on his next move before he faced B.J. It was important to handle this right, and his head was fuzzy with too much alcohol. Maybe he'd just drive back to the villa and think on it overnight before he took action.

The waitress brought his coffee, and Dana finished it slowly, wincing at its bitter taste but determined to clear his head if possible before he negotiated the narrow roads home. He thought of B.J. waiting at the villa. He wanted to hold her in his arms and tell her again how much he loved her. Whether or not her future involved IPPS or ChemCorp, he vowed to be a part of it.

Laying down a bill to cover the gratuity for the entire party who had left nothing in their sudden departure, Dana stood and walked unsteadily toward the cashier. He kept bumping into people as he made his way to the door, and he lost count of the times he apologized. As he reached the stairs, he felt quite dizzy and a man took his arm.

"Here, let me help you, sir," he said in the musical accent of the islanders.

"No, I'm—" he started to protest.

"Just show me where you are parked, sir, and I'll see you to your car."

The man had a firm grasp on his arm, and Dana felt grateful for support. He fished his keys from his pocket with his free hand and mumbled which car was his just before he passed out.

B.J. sat on the dark veranda savoring the serenity of the tropical night. The cool air of the trade wind soothed her still-sensitive skin as she breathed in the heady perfume of the blooming jasmine and listened to a mockingbird's serenade to its mate. She would miss all of this, but most of all she would miss the man who had shared this villa with her.

A tear slipped down her cheek, but she didn't bother to brush it away. What was she going to do with the rest of her life? She had succeeded in reinventing herself once but it seemed pointless to start over again when all she wanted was to love and be loved by Dana Thomas. The things that had mattered so much suddenly didn't seem to matter at all now, but it was too late to change anything. She had lost the man she loved, and she had lost her career. Surely this was as low as she could go.

The phone rang twice before it penetrated her awareness. On the fifth ring she lifted the receiver and said hello.

"Is this the residence of Mister Dana Thomas?"

After a brief pause, she answered. "Yes, but he can't come to the phone right now." She wanted to leave the impression that he was here just in case the caller was checking to see if she was alone.

"Are you Mrs. Thomas, ma'am?"

"No, I'm...no."

"This is Sergeant Steele, with the St. Croix Police. There's been an accident, ma'am. This address was in Mister Thomas' wallet, which we found discarded near the scene."

"Is Dana—what happened?" B.J. gripped the phone to stop her trembling but it didn't help.

"We found him in an alley near the Calabash where he had last been seen. He's been drugged and has a mild concussion, but he's going to be all right."

B.J. let out a breath she had not been aware of holding as she sank to the floor on legs that refused to hold her upright.

"Where is he? Can I see him?"

"He's at St. Croix Hospital, ma'am. Do you need someone

to bring you here?"

"No, I—yes, that would be good, I think." She could call one of the other men but they might not be home. She would prefer to see Dana alone anyway.

"All right, ma'am. We'll have a car at this address in about ten minutes to escort you to the hospital."

B.J. replaced the phone and hurried to put on a shirt and khaki slacks. She winced only slightly as the starched cotton brushed her tender skin. Dana was hurt and needed her. Where had he been and what had he been doing before this happened? Did it have something to do with her? She willed the cruiser to come quickly and take her to the man she loved above all else.

The arrival of the police officer and the ride to the hospital was all a blur in B.J.'s mind as she entered the lobby and was led to the emergency room.

Dana lay on a gurney with his head swathed in bandages. Wires attached to his arms led to bottles and instruments that blinked and clicked.

With a muffled sob B.J. ran to his side and bent to stroke his face. "My poor darling," she whispered.

Dana opened one eye and gave her a sleepy smile. "I'm dreaming," he croaked.

"No, you're not," she told him and placed her mouth on his for a tender kiss. "Tell me what happened?"

After a moment while he gathered his thoughts, Dana began. "I had dinner with the other guys. But they left after...a misunderstanding. Then I had a cup of coffee and that's about all I remember...until I woke up face down in a dark alley with a bump on my head."

"You were robbed, and the thugs stole your car. Thank God you're safe."

"It was worth what happened to get the answers I have now." He made an effort to focus on the woman who gazed at him with such adoration in her eyes. "You were set up. Nothing that's happened has been your fault. Frank Kelly was out for blood, and Pete Marshall went along with him."

"Can you prove that?" B.J. asked quietly, unwilling to get her hopes up for nothing.

"Absolutely. I'll take it all the way to Benny Whipple to get you vindicated if I have to."

"It doesn't matter so much anymore, Dana." She stroked his cheek. "Proving myself is not high on my priority list at the moment, but proving that I love you is."

"You've never said that you love me before." Dana shook his head. "I still feel like I'm dreaming."

"I wasn't willing to admit it, even to myself, until I thought I'd lost you."

"You never even came close. I wasn't going to let you go. Why do you think I agreed to your terms of friendship only?" He pulled her down so that her face was almost touching his.

"So you'd have someone to play golf with?"

Dana chuckled, then put his hand to his head. "That, too. So how about it? Will you be my golfing partner for life?"

"Well..." B.J. wrinkled her brow as she considered his proposal. "Single status has its perks, but I can't say no to a steady twosome."

Their lips met in a gentle kiss that sealed the future and promised fulfillment of all their dreams.

"We can get married in Christiansted as soon as I get out of here." Dana looked at her with all the love he felt in his heart. "Unless you'd prefer to have a wedding in the States?"

B.J. envisioned the lavish affair Matilda would insist upon if she had an opportunity. She shook her head. "No, a quiet island wedding would be perfect." She thought of the lovely dress and lingerie she had bought in Frederiksted and realized she had subconsciously bought her wedding trousseau already. It even included a suitable nightgown.

"We'll have to invite your sister." Dana remembered his promise made half in jest when he had found it difficult to believe Racine's hopeful prediction.

"She and my parents can fly over together when we set a date."

"I'll ask Benny Whipple to be best man." He grinned. "Though he is a proverbial confirmed bachelor." He thought of B.J.'s sister and added, "But maybe that will change."

Engrossed in their plans, they failed to hear the orderly until he spoke a second time.

"Mister Thomas?"

Dana averted his head and looked at the man who stood beside the gurney. "Yes?"

"I'm here to take you to your room. The doctor wants to admit you for observation tonight."

"I'll come with him," B.J. said.

"Are you Mrs. Thomas?" the orderly asked.

"Not yet, but close enough," B.J. answered and tucked her hand in Dana's as she fell in step beside the rolling gurney.

EPILOGUE

The wedding took place at the Buccaneer Hotel at five o'clock on a Saturday afternoon. B.J. and Dana had planned it so the sun would be setting over the blue Caribbean as they said their vows beside the fountain on The Terrace. The entire outdoor facility had been reserved for the ceremony. There was a buffet dinner and dancing afterward. This was Benny Whipple's wedding gift to the bride and groom.

B.J. was a vision in the dress she had bought in Frederiksted. Its ephemeral colors reflected her sparkling eyes and the beautiful Caribbean Sea beyond the rolling lawn of the hotel grounds.

Dana's handsome features were enhanced by the dark suit and stark white shirt he wore. His bruises were barely visible beneath his suntan.

A local priest had been commandeered for the occasion, and he spoke a charming combination of Spanish and English as he read the vows to the couple who stood before him. Finally, he pronounced them husband and wife and indicated that they should seal their commitment with a kiss.

Dana needed no urging. He opened his arms and enfolded B.J., meeting her smiling lips with a kiss so filled with love and passion that it brought sighs and tears from the watching guests. "My bride," he whispered reverently. "My love forever."

"My husband." B. J. spoke the words with pride.

The spell was broken when the guests stood and moved forward. First to speak was Benny Whipple who had been standing beside Dana as best man. With a hearty handshake that became a comradely embrace, he said in an emotional voice. "Congratulations, friend. Be happy. You deserve it."

At the same moment, B.J. and her sister Racine were

hugging and weeping joyous tears together. "Oh, what a divine wedding, Betty Jo. And this time I just know you've found the right man."

"I believe you," B.J. answered with certainty. "This time forever."

"Darlings, you are both absolutely beautiful. A mother could never be prouder than I am." Matilda Lindsey put an arm around each of her daughters and pulled them close. "Betty Jo, you are a fortunate girl to have found this man. I hope you will be very happy with him."

"I am and I will be, Mother," B.J. assured her as she turned toward her father's waiting arms.

George Lindsey gave his youngest daughter a ferocious bear hug and said in a choked voice, "Be happy, darling. You've earned the right."

B.J. pressed her lips against her father's face and tasted the salt on his cheek.

"When do I get to kiss the bride?" Benny Whipple asked.

"Right now." George released his daughter and turned toward Dana. "I want to congratulate my new son-in-law and welcome him to the family."

"Are we still on for golf tomorrow before you leave, George?"

"Wouldn't miss it," George assured him.

"Count me in, too," Benny added. "I've heard what a good game you play. Too bad we don't have a foursome."

"Oh, but we do," Dana told him. "B.J. will be playing, and she's as good as the guy who taught her."

Benny turned to Racine, who was close beside him. "Do you play, too?"

"No, but I've always wanted to learn."

"Then come along and drive my cart. Maybe I can give you a few pointers."

B.J. and Dana exchanged amused looks. Once again, Racine was expressing enthusiasm for a game she had admitted having no interest in. Obviously, her focus was on learning more about Benny and not golf.

Other guests gathered around and offered their good wishes, then wandered to the sumptuous buffet. B.J. and Dana posed for photographs with the wedding party and immediate family. The cake cutting ceremony followed, accompanied by more flashbulbs. Afterward, they attempted to eat, but the excitement of the occasion overshadowed their desire for food.

Spotting their co-workers at a table near the band, B.J. touched Dana's arm. "Let's go talk with the guys. We won't be seeing them all together again."

"Right." Dana stood and pulled out her chair. Guiding her across the terrace, he placed his hand in the hollow of her back, giving her an intimate smile when she shivered at his touch. Tonight was their wedding night, and they'd be spending it in the honeymoon suite here at the Buccaneer, thanks to her father's generous gift.

"All ready to head back to the States, Evans?"

"You bet, Thomas. And I've promised my wife I'll stay a while before I take any more overseas assignments."

"What about you, Webb? What's next on your agenda?" B.J. asked.

"I'm still thinking about the plant in China. I guess it will depend on how my wife feels about another single status job."

"Lucky you two can work together and not have to deal with that problem," Carl Evans added.

"Yes." B.J. smiled. "And I've never been to England, so I'm really looking forward to the Saltend assignment in Kingston-upon-Hull."

"That's mighty far north for winter months," Yancy Web said. "Quite a contrast to the tropics."

Dana pulled B.J. close and grinned. "But we've got our love to keep us warm."

"I wish this job could have ended well for all of us," B.J. said on a more serious note. "I'm afraid we've left a bad impression on the islanders we've worked with."

"Not at all," Albert Zurow assured her. "On the contrary, all of the IPPS people have been very professional, and as I've told you, we at ChemCorp have learned to respect a woman in the workplace because of what you've shown us. Bad people exist in every culture, and we're just happy Frank Kelley and Pete Marshall have been apprehended and will pay the consequences for their deeds."

"Well, Benny Whipple didn't wait to see the outcome of their trials before he terminated their contracts with IPPS," Webb added.

"Just bribing that club employee to kill Thomas will be

enough to send them both to prison," Desmond said.

"I don't plan to press charges," Dana said quietly. "I think they've paid for their deeds with their jobs being terminated and careers destroyed. No other company will hire them when word gets around." He gave the men a smile, pleased for their concern and support. "Besides, I have a new wife I need to be concentrating on. I want to leave this whole terrible mess behind us. If not pressing charges means we will never have to see either of those men again for a messy trial, then I'm all for it. I want my biggest concern right now to be showing off B.J. on the dance floor," he teased.

B.J. laughed and shook her head at his comment. "Thanks for coming, guys." she said to the men at the table. "We'd better get back to the other guests now. You'll stay for the dancing, won't you?"

"Wouldn't miss it, Mrs. Thomas," Lohr assured her.

B.J. felt a thrill at the sound of her name. Yes, she was Mrs. Thomas now. She looked across the terrace where her sister was leaning provocatively toward Benny Whipple.

Racine was wearing a pale yellow backless dress that clung to her in all the right places.

It was evident that the man was enchanted by her wiles. Goodbye bachelorhood. Poor man, he might be CEO of IPPS, but he didn't stand a chance against that sexy southern belle. A sudden revelation dawned on her. Her sister would probably become her boss's wife. Well, she could deal with that, knowing she had snagged the better man.

Arm in arm they left their fellow workers. As they crossed the terrace the band struck up a lively calypso tune. They paused, as all eyes on the terrace turned toward them.

Dana took a deep breath. "Shall we start the dancing?"

B.J. turned to face her handsome husband and placed her left hand on his broad shoulder. Her wedding band with its matching solitaire sparkled in the terrace lights. He folded her right hand into his palm, and pulled her closer. As their bodies touched, they began to move in perfect precision, while a silver moon rose over the dark Caribbean like a benediction.

ABOUT THE AUTHOR

Linda Swift divides her time between her native state of Kentucky and Florida. She is an award winning author of published poetry, articles, short stories, and a TV play. She has worked in public education as a teacher, counselor, and psychometrist. Her first books were published by Kensington.

She currently has available four ebooks (one in print) including a book of prose poems. She has four books of fiction, a Haiku collection, and three short stories to be released by various publishers in 2011.

Linda's supportive husband and adult children help her with all things technical. She invites you to stop by her website at www.lindaswift.net.